MARAUDERS OF THE
ROSWELL LINKS

MARAUDERS OF THE ROSWELL LINKS

Code Name: QFTAMC
Episode I

Science Fiction

Joshua K. Alam

iUniverse, Inc.
New York Bloomington Shanghai

MARAUDERS OF THE ROSWELL LINKS
Code Name: QFTAMC Episode I

iUniverse books may be ordered through booksellers or by contacting:

iUniverse
1663 Liberty Drive
Bloomington, IN 47403
www.iuniverse.com
1-800-Authors (1-800-288-4677)

Because of the dynamic nature of the Internet, any Web addresses or links contained in this book may have changed since publication and may no longer be valid.

This is a work of fiction. All of the characters, names, incidents, organizations, and dialogue in this novel are either the products of the author's imagination or are used fictitiously.

Library of Congress Registration Number:
TXU 1-363-222

ISBN: 978-0-595-49178-0 (pbk)
ISBN: 978-0-595-60995-6 (ebk)

Printed in the United States of America

Contents

CHAPTER 1

CRASH LANDING—322 B. C.

A sleek spaceship glided gracefully through the interplanetary space of the solar system of planet Earth. The spacecraft was not from the planet Earth because Earth's civilization was still in the early stages of its technology. The crew, four alien life forms, seemed to be content and comfortable inside the command control section of the space ship.

With strange, loud, humming sounds the ship started to shake. The beings in the control room quickly moved around and pressed with precision various control buttons. The brightly-lit consul spouted lights of all colors. The crew seemed worried, but worked calmly; checking different panels and pressing different command buttons to stabilize the shaking ship that had now started to lose altitude. With a loud crackling noise, one of the control panels started to melt and burn. The crew quickly sprayed fire retardant substance on the panel, which stopped the fire. The ship shook violently, then lost its graceful glide and plunged downward as the Earth's gravitational force pulled it down.

Eliezer Abishu awakened before dawn, to take his daily morning walk, as he had done all his life. He lived on the outskirts of the town, Ramah. The sky was still lit up with bright stars. As he walked he heard a strange, thundering noise. He looked up and saw a bright object falling from the sky. This was not new to him, since he had seen shooting stars fall toward the earth before. However this shooting star was a bit different. He noticed that the falling star stopped falling and started to circulate over a small hill. It seemed as if the falling object was trying to stop its fall and fly back up. And then the object disappeared behind the hill.

Eliezer was scared and curious; his curiosity prevailed and he cautiously moved closer to see the fallen object. As he moved closer, to his surprise he saw a huge object with blinking lights of many colors, which were clouded by rising smoke. The spaceship skidded against the hill before coming to a stop. Eliezer froze in his tracks. He had never seen or heard of such a thing. He was frightened, but could not resist his curiosity, so he slowly and cautiously moved closer to the object.

At a closer look the object seemed to be made of some kind of gray colored metal that he had never seen before. It looked like a small house. Eliezer could see it clearly now because the early morning sun had begun to rise. Eliezer saw a small door on the side of the object open up and a lot of smoke pouring out. A strange being staggered out of the opening pulling another being, slightly smaller than himself.

They were both dressed in strange clothes. The smaller being seemed to be hurt and was not moving. They had colorful patches and pictures of strange stars and metal objects, like their space ship, on their garments. They both wore strange headgear with clear, glass pieces that covered their faces. The glass type material of the headgear of the small being had been torn off and the face was no longer covered. Eliezer saw that that being had almost the same features as humans, but different. The being that pulled the other being seemed upset. He was so busy trying to revive his friend that he did not even notice Eliezer who was only a few feet from him, but when the being noticed him, Eliezer felt a tingly feelings in his brain, as though someone was trying to talk to him. There was no sound, but Eliezer realized that the being was talking to him without speaking.

Now Eliezer was really scared. He was ready to run away when he heard the alien. "Do not be afraid of us. We need your help."

"How can I hear you?" Eliezer asked. "You don't talk or make a sound?"

"I am communicating through telepathy—through thought transmission and thought reception. It is something like mind reading. In this way we do not have to learn hundreds of languages when we visit other planets," the alien explained and added, "And of course I am able to make these references by reading your thoughts. You have many languages on your world. We use to have many different languages on our planet long, long ago. I could talk if I have to but it is very uncomfortable for me to communicate my thoughts through oral sounds, it is like forcing your intelligent sea creatures, like dolphins to speak."

"It is very strange and foreign to me," Eliezer said, "But I am glad that we can communicate.... Please tell me what this metal house is?"

"We call it a space ship," the alien replied, "It can fly and take us from planet to planet and star to star any where in the space, you call skies"

"Are you telling me that this metal house can fly and that you are from another world?"

The alien replied, "We have come from a world far away. My home world consists of twenty—eight sister planets and two stars or what you call suns. Our ship has crashed and my life companion is badly hurt. Two of my crew members are no longer alive."

"Do you have males and females in your world?" Eliezer asked.

The alien replied, "Yes. She is my companion for life, just like when you get married. She is badly hurt. Not only that but her headgear is smashed which helps us to breathe and stay alive on foreign planets."

The alien's companion started to move. The alien looked happy and communicated back with Eliezer. "My companion is feeling better. It seems that your atmosphere is very similar to ours and she is able to breathe without any special breathing mechanism in your atmosphere and stay alive."

The alien then communicated to his mate, who nodded her head. He went into his space ship and returned with a box that had an instrument in it, which he waved in the air.

He seemed pleased with the results. He then gently took the broken helmet off of his mate. Her forehead was bleeding. The morning breeze made her gain consciousness quickly, but she still seemed weak. Eliezer noticed that she had beautiful, human-like features, except she did not have ears or hair. She had shiny copper colored skin.

"Is there anything I can do?" Eliezer asked.

"Her bleeding must be stopped or she will cease to exist. Our medicine supplies have been destroyed in the crash."

"With your permission I might be able to help," Eliezer said.

The male alien seemed hesitant as he communicated with his mate. Eliezer noticed that she gave the male alien a comforting smile and nodded her head gently as to agree to get help from him. "Thank you," the male alien said, "We trust that you want to help us…. We have no other alternative."

Eliezer cleared some dust from a face of a rock. He then tore off a cloth from his silk garment. He burnt it on the rock that he had cleared of dust. "This is an old remedy that I have learned from my grandmother," Eliezer said. "I have burnt the silk from my garment and now I will pack the ashes into her wound."

"I would like to analyze the ashes first," the alien said. The alien tested the ashes with tools from his box. "These ashes are silicon-based. We are a silicon-based life form. This may help."

Eliezer gathered the ashes and packed it into the wound. The bleeding stopped.

"She will need rest and nourishment to gain her strength," Eliezer said.

The alien replied, "I am grateful for your help." He added, "Would you like to come inside my space ship to see it?"

Eliezer was a little hesitant, but said, "Yes, I would like to see your space ship."

The alien helped his mate back into the ship. The smoke had cleared out. Inside the ship the atmosphere was cool, while outside it was getting warm. The alien's mate, instead of lying down on a bed-like structure, wanted to sit in the chair in front of the ship's computer control panel where some lights were blinking. She opened and shut some panels and checked buttons and switches. She looked very worried. Her mate also looked worried.

Eliezer asked, "Is there a problem?"

The alien replied, "Yes. We have a big problem. Most of our ship's energy packs have been destroyed. This means that our space ship cannot fly. We can not leave your world."

Eliezer moved closer to the control panels. All of a sudden the blinking lights on the control panels started to blink brighter. The alien and his mate's eyes grew wide in surprise. "What did I do?" Eliezer asked, "Did I touch something? Why are the lights blinking faster?"

"You have done nothing wrong, my brother from another world. It seems that you have something that is affecting our energy packs and perhaps increasing their energy output …"

The alien's mate had finally gained the strength to communicate. She said, "I thank you for your help. I feel my strength returning." Looking at the control panel she said, "You seem to be affecting our energy packs.... We do not want to be too optimistic only to be disappointed. We want to be sure that this is not just an anomaly, so please move away from the control panels and then move back closer."

Eliezer smiled, "Ah ... There is an old saying, 'A wise woman is like a treasure.'"

He moved back and then closer to the control panel ... As he got closer to the control panels again the lights grew brighter. Both aliens looked happy.

The alien said, "We are positive that you have something that is increasing the energy in our modules."

Eliezer replied, "If it helps you to get your spaceship fixed and get back to your world, I'll do anything to help you. You are my friends from another world."

"My mate and I are both very thankful and impressed by your friendship for us."

The alien's mate said, "I would like to tell you of a legend. In our world there is a legend ... Tens of thousands of years ago some of our ancestor space travelers left our world to explore other worlds. Some of those space travelers did not return for a long time. They were gone ... Communication was received from them for a time but then the communication stopped forever. We don't know what world they settled in.... It could even have been Earth ... But enough of old legends." The alien's mate smiled. "We must figure out what it is about you that is creating energy when you come near the control panel. Perhaps it is the shiny rocks around your neck that are increasing the energy levels of our energy packs. Can we use them? I must warn you that they might get destroyed."

Eliezer was hesitant. "These are diamonds. My wife gave this necklace to me on our wedding day. I always wear it. It is very valuable to me." Eliezer wanted to help the aliens so he said, "You may use it if it will help you repair your ship." He took the necklace off and gave it to the male alien. He thought to himself that his wife would think he was a fool, but he knew the importance of these aliens returning to their own world. He said to the aliens, "My wife will think me a fool for giving away her wedding gift, but I will try to explain to her."

"Thank you, and our apologies for taking something so valuable from you."

The male alien took the diamond necklace from Eliezer and gave it to his mate. She took the diamonds off very carefully and put them into a small box, and then turned a switch on the box. A sharp noise came out of the box, which was similar to the noise when a metal tool is sharpened on a limestone wheel. After a little while the noise stopped and the female alien turned off the switch and opened the box. Eliezer looked in the box in amazement when he saw that the diamonds were all cut into different geometrical shapes to fit into the panel.

The female alien took them out of the box and slid them into the panels after taking out the charred and cracked energy packs. As soon as the diamond modules were placed into the panels there was a slight humming sound and then all the panel lights lit up in bright colors. The female alien looked very happy. She checked a lot of buttons and checked the readings that came up on the command control. "It has worked!" she said, "Every thing is back to normal. The ship's engines and controls are working." Looking at Eliezer she said, "We are very thankful to you. Would you like to fly in our ship? My mate and I would like to show you how this ship flies."

Eliezer was nervous, but also curious so he somewhat bravely said, "Yes I would."

The male alien pointed to an empty seat of one of his crew members that had died in the crash and said, "Sit down and strap yourself in, like me." Eliezer sat down and tried to strap himself in by following the way the alien strapped himself in, but he had a little problem because he was not used to it. The alien smiled and helped him. Once every one was strapped down, the alien and his mate pressed some buttons and many bright lights and screens light up on the command control. The ship engines made a low humming sound and the ship lifted off.

Images of the space ship appeared on many screens as it flew over deserts, oceans, valleys and mountains. He flew over land that Eliezer had never seen before, but had heard of. Also, to his surprise, on one screen he saw pictures of his village and his people. He saw his household—his wife and his children. He could hear their voices as if they were standing next to him, as his wife got them ready for their daily chores. "How did you get my wife and children into your spaceship?" Eliezer asked.

"These are images of your family. They are safe in the village where you left them.

"Am I really seeing my household?" Eliezer asked.

"Yes, you are seeing them as they go about their day."

Eliezer noticed that his wife seemed worried, and prayed for his safety. The male alien told Eliezer that he would communicate with her to reassure her that Eliezer was safe, was helping his friends, and would be home soon. His wife trusted this knowledge; she understood that he was safe. It was not the first time that he had been delayed while helping people in need. Eliezer could see that she was no longer worried.

The alien explained further, "With our instruments we can see any part of your world on our screen." The spaceship flew over the ocean. The alien commented, "We have great bodies of water, trees and mountains like this in our home world also. It is amazing how similar our worlds are. Now we are going to find shiny rocks like yours so we can replace your rocks. We know that they were given to you by your life mate and they are important to you."

The female alien pressed some keys on the control panels and an image of diamonds appeared on the screen. The spaceship flew again over mountains and valleys and came to a beautiful strange land. The spaceship stopped in mid-air over a hill and the images of diamonds buried under a layer of clay and rock appeared on the screen. The alien's mate pressed a button and deposits of diamond disappeared from the ground below and then appeared in a different section of the space ship.

Eliezer told them to collect silver and gold also, so they collected gold and silver in the same way. Eliezer asked where the diamonds, gold and silver had been stored and the alien told Eliezer to follow him. The alien pressed a button on one of the panels and a door opened in the side of the command control section. Eliezer followed him through that door and came to room where he saw the diamonds, gold and silver piled separately.

Eliezer had some knowledge to determine the quality of precious metals and diamonds. He found that everything was of a very high quality.

The alien said, "We are going to need the shiny rocks so we are going to take half of them to make sure that we have enough energy for our space ship. The metals you call gold and silver we have no use for so we are going to take a very small amount of that just to show our people different types of substances found in your world. You can have the rest."

"Thank you for all the riches that you have brought," Eliezer exclaimed, "This reminds me of a saying we have in my world, 'Good deeds are always rewarded.'"

"We are eternally in your debt, my brother from another world," the alien replied, "Now let us go back to the control room so we can take you back to your homeland."

"I can not wait to tell my wife about this and show her all the riches," Eliezer said, "Of course I can not share this with every one because they will not believe it."

The alien and Eliezer went back to the control room where the female alien was waiting for them. They both strapped themselves into the seats. The female alien pressed some buttons and the ship began to fly. Eliezer looked at the control screens. The ship flew over land and sea. Eliezer saw strange herds of land animals, sea creatures and vegetation. In a short period of time the spaceship landed back in the same valley where they had left.

The alien said, "Our home world looked similar to your home world. I have seen it in our planet history files."

Eliezer replied, "We are kin from different worlds."

"Yes," the alien said, "I feel a kinship to you."

When they were disembarking the alien asked, "How should we transport these treasures to your home?"

Eliezer replied, "I could bring my ox cart and load up and take it … But someone could follow me and see us and bring some calamity on me, and my family, by accusing me of dealing with strange beings. My people are very backward. Everyone is not as accepting of others as I am.… The best thing would be that after I get home you talk to me through telepathy. I will show you a safe room in my house and you put it there."

"We will do exactly according to your instructions," the alien said. "Once again thank you for trusting us with your treasure. We know how much you want this treasure. But before we part we want to show you our appreciation for helping us. We would like to share our knowledge with you."

The alien's mate said, "I am the spaceship's science and technology expert. I have prepared a condensed knowledge and learning device in your language and your way of learning and teaching by using the thought patterns of your brain. It provides step by step instructions to learn the basics of complex concepts of our knowledge. Teach this knowledge to your children and your children's children, so your future generations will be able to solve the mysteries of space."

She gave Eliezer a small gray box with two buttons on the side, a black button and a red button. The box had a screen like the screens in the control command center. She pressed the black button and a small panel slid out of the stem of the box that had different colored buttons. Some buttons had images of arrows that the female alien explained were directional commands. The gray square box was no bigger than two lengths of his palm. It was made of a strange substance and was very light in weight. She showed Eliezer how everything worked.

"Eliezer, when you press the black button on the side it turns the instructor module on, and if you press it again it turns it off and the panel slides back in. Go ahead, press the black button."

Eliezer pressed the black button. The screen lit up and the command panel slid out at the stem of the instructional module. The screen diagrammed the different colored buttons' functions. Some buttons represented different subject areas and order of knowledge. Eliezer presses the purple button. It projects knowledge of math—algebra, geometry—starting with the simplest one-digit numbers to highly complex computations that Eliezer did not understand. The green button projected information about the planet, such as the earth, its' oceans, and different life forms on the planet. The blue button projected knowledge about space—the stars, planets, galaxies, universe and space ships and space travel. The white button projected knowledge about medicine. Another button projected knowledge about strange weapons, and there were many other buttons and orders of knowledge. Eliezer was surprised and awed that all that knowledge could be contained in one small box.

Reading his thoughts the female alien took out a small diamond crystal from the back slot of the instructor module. "All the knowledge is stored, not in the box, but on this tiny diamond crystal. Be sure that you pass this knowledge onto your children. All your children. I have learned from your thoughts that you do not let your female children learn and excel like your male children. Make sure that the female children have the same opportunity to gain knowledge. Make sure that anyone, regardless of their gender, race, beliefs, color or customs, who wants to learn, has the opportunity to learn from you. Learning and knowledge helps us to be free from the fears of the unknown and brings living beings closer to understand each other. Remember that a world civilization that is rich in learning and knowledge is a civilization that would endure through any kind of dangers and tribulations."

"I am grateful for the knowledge that you have entrusted me with," Eliezer said, "I will make sure that my people, male and female learn this knowledge."

The alien said, "Eliezer, with this knowledge you will be able to build remarkable machines that will fly you from one end of your world to the other and far and beyond through space, like us. You will be able to grow an abundant amount of food, make amazing medicine to cure sickness, and prolong life beyond your imagination. With this knowledge you will be able to make weapons and will have the power to destroy, defend and protect yourself against invaders from your home world and invaders who might drift into your solar system from other worlds. Invaders from other solar systems may have the ambition and technological means to dominate less developed life forms and the power to annihilate worlds. We know many aggressive and violent life forms in the universe; one of the worst is called the Pirons, of the deep northern galactic cluster, who have dominated and destroyed many worlds. They almost destroyed us. The only time you should use the destructive power from this knowledge is to defend and protect yourself against aggressors. Do not use this knowledge and power to conquer and subdue others. Use this knowledge to unite your race and excel in the knowledge as a united race, so you do not self-destruct. I have seen it happen to many worlds where inhabitants of those worlds use knowledge to destroy one another and we have seen their lifeless, baron wasteland of worlds floating aimlessly in space. Do not let this happen to your world."

The female alien continued, "Once your race has learned this knowledge you will be able to build on that knowledge and you will be able to go beyond it. You will be able to solve the mysteries of the universe. Everything is in your hands."

She continued, "Eliezer, whenever you have a problem with this instructional and knowledge module, or you want to get in touch with us, press the red button and we will get in touch with you."

When it was time to leave, Eliezer, with a great sadness in his voice, said, "Will I ever see you again?"

"That is difficult to say," The female alien said, "The part of the galaxy, in which your star system is located, is considered undeveloped and uncharted. You have maps to go from one place to another. We have something similar but it gives us information on how to travel to different parts of the galaxy and universe. This information is placed in the command control modules of our space ships and when we want to go some place in the universe, we punch in that location and our spaceships are guided to those destinations. Our command control memory unit got jammed and locked when we crashed. Because of that we cannot chart in the location of this new star system, (your star system). It does not already exist in the memory units. You will learn more about this knowledge and beyond. I have put all this and more information on your knowledge and instructional module."

"I can not even hope that some day you will return?" Eliezer asked.

"You should never lose hope," the female alien said, "I have set the red button function on an automatic one million of your miles distance sensitive mode. It means that if our space ship is passing through this quadrant of the galaxy and is at a distance of one million miles from your world, the red button will automatically start sending signals (by beeping and blinking) to our space ship. Then you will know that we are close by and will be able to locate our brother's home world out of millions of planets scattered in your part of the galaxy, and we will communicate with you through telepathy. Make sure to take good care of the knowledge module."

"If you are millions of miles away how will you get my message right away when I send a signal from my world?" Eliezer asked.

The female alien said with a smile, "My brother, that is a good question. You will learn more about space travel and more once you study the knowledge module. It works something like this. When you press the red knob it generates an ultra hyper special power-transmission, which allows the tiny energy particles carrying your signal to hop on other tiny particles that are already in motion and continue to hop from one particle to the next moving forward, which allows your signal to move forward faster and faster toward its destination in a short period of time until it reaches its destination. In this case the destination will be our receiver and us. We will answer back the same way. Also, your module is set to transmit signals on a special frequency exclusively for your instructional and knowledge box and our receiver, so only our receiver will receive your message. This is to safe guard against other life forms in the galaxy or the universe picking up your signal, and coming to look for you. If you learn the knowledge we are leaving with you, you will be able to understand these concepts and more in no time."

"You are truly a great teacher," Eliezer said.

"And you are very intelligent for someone from Earth, my brother."

Eliezer took the box of knowledge and instructions and went home. He told his wife and children that he was all right and went to the room that he had built under his house to hide his family when in danger. He asked the aliens to move his share of diamonds, gold and silver to that room. The treasure from the space ship appeared in that room.

He heard the aliens say, "Goodbye dear friend and kin brother from another world. We will never forget your kindness. We are leaving now."

Eliezer replied, "Goodbye my friends and kin from another world. May God bless you with a safe journey home. I shall always remember your advice and teach the knowledge that you have left with me to my people and anyone else who would like to learn." Eliezer felt no communication in his mind. He knew that the aliens were gone.

❧   ❧   ❧

Eliezer showed the treasure to his wife, which made her very happy.

The first thing that Eliezer did was to open a school where all children, male and female, young and old, any one from near and far could go for a minimal fee. If someone could not afford the fee, they were given special assistance to be able to attend his school. Eliezer made sure that no one was turned away. The reason Eliezer and his wife charged a fee was to make sure that no one suspected them of finding a treasure, and also to make the students value learning since they had to pay for their education.

In a short period of time the fame of his excellent school and great knowledge spread from city to city and kingdom to kingdom. People came in great numbers to attend his school. Everyone who came to his school was impressed by the amazing new knowledge.

Eliezer and his wife had to hire apprentices and assistants to instruct the masses. He wrote a detailed description of various star systems, highly advanced information about scientific, geometrical, mathematical equations, and space travel. He wrote about strange weapons, and knowledge to perform medical miracles. He wrote as much as he could remember from the instruction and knowledge module that the aliens had given him.

Eliezer and his wife wrote down step-by-step instructions on countless parchments for beginner and advance learners. Assistant-instructors were given sets of parchments to keep in their instructional rooms so everyone had free access to those parchments. Eliezer's sons and daughters, at his father's instruction, oversaw and made sure that anyone who wanted to use the parchments had the opportunity to do so. So with their father and mother's approval they built a great library for those who were not attending the school.

They were able to gain knowledge during their free time. Eliezer remembered that the aliens said to make the knowledge available for everyone who seeks it. Eliezer became the adviser to many tribal leaders and kings. Years passed by and Eliezer, his wife and his children grew stronger in their new knowledge. Every one who met with them marveled at their wisdom and intellect.

Eliezer always kept the module box of knowledge and instruction clean, dry and away from sand and dust particles. He kept it close—in his robe pocket. His wife had sewn bigger pockets in his robes to accommodate that box. Eliezer communicated with the aliens now and then when he needed an explanation about a concept of knowledge he did not understand. The aliens were always happy to communicate with him.

One day, one of the assistant-instructors, who respected Eliezer very much, wanted to show his respect and gratitude to Eliezer and so decided to wash the robe that Eliezer has taken off to take a bath. The assistant took the robe off the peg, where it had been neatly hanging and put the robe in boiling hot water. When the assistant removed the robe to wring it, and spread it to dry, he heard strange, crackling, hissing and beeping noises coming from the robe. The assistant saw a bulge in the robe and he thought it was a snake that has gotten into the robe. The assistant picked up a heavy staff and started hitting the bulging spot on the robe. Eliezer, after finishing his bath, wrapped in a towel, realized that his robe with the knowledge module box in the pocket was missing. He hurried to his office chamber and saw his assistant hitting the robe with a heavy staff. Eliezer grabbed the staff away from his assistant.

"Did I not tell you to not go into my office chamber and touch my things?" Eliezer screamed in an unparalleled rage that his assistant had never seen before.

The assistant replied, "Yes my lord, you have. I was just trying to wash your robe to show my gratitude, but I heard strange noises and I thought that there was a poisonous snake in your robe. I tried to kill it, so it would not harm you. I'm sorry if I have angered you."

Eliezer, being wise and knowing what was done could not be undone, said, "I am sorry that I raised my voice. We all make mistakes."

Eliezer brought the robe into his office and checked the box. It was broken into many pieces, but the small diamond crystal about the size of a square-inch was not even scratched. Eliezer told his wife and his sons what has happened and after unsuccessfully trying to contact the aliens, they put all the pieces and the small crystal in a velvet lined container made out of strong metal and kept it safely with other treasures, hoping that someday, from the knowledge already learned and written on parchments, his offspring would be able to fix the instructions and knowledge module. Eliezer and his wife also hoped that maybe the aliens would come back and try to find them and help fix the instructions and knowledge box. But Eliezer knew deep down in his heart that it would not happen unless there was a miracle because the aliens could not locate their world without the signals from the instruction and knowledge box.

Eliezer thought, with tears rolling down his cheeks, "I am so sorry my alien kin. I lost all the knowledge that you have trusted me with. Most of all, I will not be able to communicate with you. May God bless you and keep you safe whereever you are."

Eliezer decided to write down a detailed and full account of his encounter with the aliens. He also wrote down where he kept the broken pieces of the knowledge module, along with the little diamond crystal.

Eliezer continued to teach and spread knowledge. His school continued to grow. His children and his children's' children continue with the tradition of spreading knowledge, in the same tradition that Eliezer and his wife did. Many generations passed.

The day came when invading soldiers and their legions took over the land. The buildings of the great school that Eliezer had started lay in ruins. Eliezer's great, great grand children hid the box that contained the broken pieces of the instruction and knowledge module along with the diamond crystal that powered the little box that their great, great grand father had received from the aliens. They also hid gold and silver treasures with the box.

CHAPTER 2

PARCHMENTS DISCOVERED YEAR 2000

Two male tourists traveling through the desert got separated from their group in a sandstorm and lost their way. When the sandstorm ended they tried to find their way back to their group, but they got lost even further.

The desert is unkind; its sand dunes change with every sandstorm and flow of wind. One great dune might be here today but moved by the winds somewhere else tomorrow. The desert does not keep your footprints; you cannot back-track your way. Here are words of wisdom for the lost and the wanderer, "Do not stand still in the desert when the high winds blow, or you are doomed."

While they searched their way back, the men came upon the ruins of a building unearthed by the sandstorm. One of the tourists leaned against a wall of the building to rest, but under his weight the middle of the wall crumbled. He saw papyrus parchment scrolls sticking out of the walls. Curiously, both men tore more of the wall and discovered a great number of these parchments. There were so many parchments that they would have needed a truck to carry them all. They quickly picked up some of the parchment scrolls and fit them in their backpacks. They marked the area by tying a red bandanna on a stick and began again to search their way back.

When the sandstorm ended, their tour group sent search helicopters to find them. It was late in the afternoon when one of the helicopters located them and picked them up. While in the helicopter the tourists relayed what they had found in the old ruins. They told the whole crowd that gathered to greet them how they had discovered the scrolls. It made the evening news headlines. The scrolls were immediately purchased and secured by a museum. The next day when the authorities and the museum workers, along with the two tourists, went to pick up the rest of the parchments, they could not find a single one. Every thing had been swept clean, except the red bandanna tied to a stick. Apparently someone had picked up all the parchments during the night.

A few days later the curators of the museum published a small article in a newspaper saying that the parchments that the tourists found were authentic. The language style and carbon readings of the parchment showed that they were over two thousands years old. The article also noted that one of the parchments mentioned a "Treasure Map" and a small box believed to contain a diamond crystal that held great powers. The box was believed to have been given to a man named Eliezer, by aliens from outer space. These beings supposedly could talk without speaking, had great powers, and befriended Eliezer, giving him this little box of knowledge. This box supposedly contained a wealth of knowledge about technology, science and many other disciplines. It was said that by mistake the box was broken down to pieces by one of Eliezer's assistants. The news article further reported that this story or legend had been passed down from generation to generation, but the map and box had been lost for many thousands of years.

On an exclusive Mediterranean Island, Michael Kavanaugh, the reclusive billionaire, who owned a string of islands in the Mediterranean, sat in his study. The study was on the fourth floor of a massive fortified, concrete building. It was tastefully decorated with tapestries, priceless artwork and paintings by world known artists. A huge mahogany conference table surrounded by mahogany chairs occupied the middle of the room. On the table sat a state-of-the—art computer.

In his spacious king-sized chair, Michael Kavanaugh sat staring at the computer screen. On his right flashed computer monitors—his link to the outside world. He used electronic technology to control his empire. Small groups of important subordinates occupied offices surrounding his spacious study. His island was filled with a small army of technicians and employees. Each one of these employees, (who had earned the right to work with Kavanaugh), were the best in their profession.

"Mr. Kavanaugh, Mr. DeLoatch is here to see you," Kavanaugh's receptionist said over the intercom.

"Send him in," Kavanaugh replied.

The elevator door opened at the end of the study and Bernard DeLoatch walked in. Bernard DeLoatch, a well-built man, was a little over six feet tall, with short cropped light-brown hair and a thin mustache. He was France's most ruthless and well known international smuggler and dealer of illegal arms. He was the contact person for assassination arrangements—of any one—at the right price. He also smuggled valuable and rare, stolen artifacts and art works.

"Mr. Kavanaugh, you wanted to see me?" Bernard DeLoatch asked.

Kavanaugh replied, "There has been talk of the discovery of ancient parchments and an ancient map that shows the location of a great treasure and a diamond crystal that powers a small box of knowledge. This box was given to a man over 2,000 years ago by some strange aliens from another world."

"Mr. Kavanaugh, I have heard of this story. This is a story or a legend that has been passed around in certain families—Man's age-old desire to fly and go to different worlds. Not long ago a similar type of story had been circling around that aliens had landed in Roswell, New Mexico."

The unscrupulous billionaire told the notorious ancient artifact smuggler, "The Roswell incident is not the only link that shows us that aliens have landed on earth in the past. Myths, legends and many unexplainable wonders are scattered around the planet Earth, providing links that aliens have visited our planet.

"The parchments that were brought to the museum talk about a map, but the map was not with those parchments. The rest of the parchments were stolen before the authorities and the museum people got to them. Do you know or can you find out who took the rest of the parchments from those ruins?"

"I know who took rest of the parchments. I keep myself abreast of this kind of thing. The person who took the rest of the parchments is Sheik Farooque. He is the man who got the means and the connections to steal and sell each one of those parchments in the black market at a handsome price."

"I want you to get that map," Kavanaugh said, "With that map, I want you to find that container that holds the diamond crystal and broken pieces of that ancient box mentioned in the map. Bring those items to me, and eliminate any one who is also after that map. Money is no object."

Bernard DeLoatch replied, "Let's say that we start out with twenty million dollars, plus expenses. Half of the money should be transferred in advance to my Swiss account that has been given to your accountants, and if the operation gets complicated there will be additional charges."

"As I have told you," Kavanaugh said, "Money is no object. In the future, we will not meet each other unless it is extremely necessary. You will be contacted when needed. If you wish to contact me, leave a message with my special assistant in Paris, and someone will get in touch with me."

"Agreed," De Loatch said and he walked back to the elevator. Kavanaugh pressed a button on his desk, the elevator door opened, and Bernard DeLoatch left.

※   ※   ※

The Interpol chief, Donald Klein, kept a close watch on Bernard DeLoatch. The Interpol had picked up an urgent communication that Bernard DeLoatch wanted to meet with Sheik Farooque. They were to meet at Farooque's office in Cairo, Egypt the next day at 5:00 p.m. after Farooque's workers left.

Sheik Farooque was another notorious and unscrupulous, well-to-do dealer of rare, valuable and collectable artifacts. This served as a front to hide his illegal black market business deals, which included international, illegal arms shipments and more.

Donald Klein asked Mr. Roger Grace, (Chief of the American based Global Intelligence Services—GIS), if agent Robert Kirkland could be used for a short mission. Klein wanted Kirkland to pose as Bernard DeLoatch and meet with Sheik Farooque to find out what was going on.

Robert Kirkland was an American agent for the GIS, who was based in France. He had worked with Donald Klein on many occasions. Kirkland had a similar appearance to DeLoatch, except for the thin mustache, which was easily remedied. Once he placed the mustache on, no one could tell the difference between Bernard DeLoatch and himself.

Kirkland picked up the information from the Interpol office and got on the airplane destined to Cairo. At the Cairo Airport, his long time friend, Sullimon, was waiting for him. Sullimon also worked for the American embassy.

"Robert it is good to see you," Sullimon said, "The mustache looks good on you. I think you should grow one like that."

"Good to see you too, Sullimon," Kirkland replied, "I like this red sports car of yours. Some rich uncle died?"

"The Interpol guys left this little red car for the mission. I have to return it by tomorrow," Sullimon laughed and then frowned, "I don't like the way this is set up. We go in early, meet with the sheik while the Interpol stalls Bernard DeLoatch?"

"That's the plan."

"Robert, suppose the Interpol cannot stall Bernard DeLoatch? Why couldn't the Interpol pick up Bernard DeLoatch for something, and let him out when we are out safe?"

"I wish it could have been done like that," Kirkland replied, "But then they would have become suspicious. And you know these high level crooks. They operate in the dark gray areas of what is considered legal and illegal. You can't just pick 'em up and handhold them."

"Do you have any idea why DeLoatch is meeting with Farooque?" Sullimon asked.

"That is the purpose of this mission—to find out what they are meeting about. I believe this meeting is about the illegal sale of arms to small countries."

"O.K.," Sullimon said, "Let's just get it done. I agreed to the mission because of you. If it were some other agent I would have made up some excuse to get out of this assignment."

"Thanks Sullimon," Kirkland said, "Now remember if things get out of control, take off."

"You know that I won't do that," Sullimon replied, "We're in this together. We finish together."

They arrived about 4:15 at Sheik Farooque's office building. It was a luxurious, two story ultra-modern complex, located in the beautiful, suburban part of Cairo. Meetings were held on the first floor, in a spacious office. Sullimon waited outside, in the parking lot, which was not far from the office building entrance. Robert Kirkland did not have any problem getting in.

"Aslam-a-Lackum," Sheik Farooque said to Kirkland when Kirkland entered looking like DeLoatch. Kirkland knew this to be an Arabic greeting. Farooque continued, "Mr. DeLoatch, it is a pleasant surprise to see you come personally to my humble dwelling."

"Thanks, Sheik Farooque," Kirkland replied, "I know that you are a busy man, so I would like you to come right to the point."

"As you wish," Farooque said, "It is my understanding that you are searching for a special parchment that has a map drawn on it along with the broken pieces of a box made out of strange substance, and a diamond crystal. It is mentioned that the box was given to a person by some strange beings, maybe from another world."

Kirkland was caught off guard about the mention of an old map. He had thought that the meeting was about some kind of illegal arms shipments, however he composed himself. "Oh, yes the ancient map. I would like to purchase it."

"The price is one million dollars," Sheik Farooque said and gave Robert Kirkland an account number on a piece of paper. "When one million dollars are deposited in that account, the authentic map will be delivered immediately."

"I would like to see the map to make sure that it is authentic," Kirkland said. Indignant, Sheik Farooque said, "Mr. DeLoatch, I do not make bad deals. I would not have any objection to show you the map if I had it here. For security reasons, so it does not get stolen, the map is safely kept with a friend and business associate of mine." Farooque looked at Robert Kirkland doubtfully. He did not like to be mistrusted in his business deals. There is honor among crooks and their criminal code.

A phone on Sheik Farooque's table rang. It was one of his security guards calling from the entrance gate asking to let Bernard DeLoatch and his associates in. Sheik Farooque looked at Kirkland and realized that he was a fake. He replied to the security guard on the phone, "Yes. Let him in."

Robert Kirkland saw a look of caution spread across Sheik Farooque's face. A warning instrument in his pants pocket shook, which meant big trouble. "Get out of here now," Kirkland thought, "Something has gone wrong." Kirkland saw two big, luxury cars pulling into the parking lot. He also saw Sheik Farooque nonchalantly looking for something in his drawer. Kirkland quickly took out his gun and pointed it at Sheik Farooque saying quietly, "Put your hands on the table, now."

Sheik Farooque took his hands out of the drawer, a gun in his hand. He gently dropped the gun and put his hands on the table. "Who are you?" Sheik Farooque asked, "Let's talk."

Robert Kirkland ignored the question. He knew that Sheik Farooque was trying to delay. Kirkland reached over while still pointing the gun at Farooque and picked the gun off the table, saying, "Which way out?"

With a cunning smile, Sheik Farooque pointed toward a door behind his chair.

"You first," Kirkland said. Sheik Farooque did not move. Robert Kirkland figured it led to some deadly trap. He had to think fast. Time was running out. He heard many footsteps. Kirkland crashed through a big bay window into some bushes and as he did he glimpsed three big men and the real Bernard DeLoatch entering the room.

"Stop him!" Sheik Farooque yelled.

Sullimon drove right through the bushes as he saw Robert Kirkland crashing through the window. DeLoatch and his henchmen shot at Kirkland. Sullimon opened the passenger side of the door and shot back at DeLoatch and his gang. Some of the gang members were now out of the building. They yelled, ran and shot at Kirkland. Robert Kirkland was just a few feet away from the car when he felt a bullet hit him in the right leg and another bullet in the back. His right leg went limp. He could not move forward and he fell to the ground. Sullimon reached across the car to the passenger door, grabbed Kirkland and pulled him in the car and they took off.

"Sullimon, what are you doing? I had told you to not risk your life," Kirkland whispered, "I am not going to make it." He looked at his right leg. Part of it was blown apart.

The red sports sedan, which carried Sullimon and Kirkland, raced on a narrow road chased by its pursuers, two big luxury cars. The constant spray of machine-gun bullets and automatic assault rifle bullets from the pursuers made it very difficult for Sullimon to dodge. Luckily it was an abandoned road. There was gunfire, shooting and the screeching noise of car wheels during this high-speed chase, (although it was not all that unusual to have a high speed car chase, shoot outs and gunfire exchanges between rival groups in this beautiful city, Cairo).

The thick clouds that covered the sky made visibility low. Heavy rain, that just started, made it even harder to drive fast, weave and dodge oncoming bullets.

Sullimon looked at his longtime friend, Robert Kirkland, who had been shot in the right leg and back, and was in need of serious medical attention. Sullimon listened hopefully for the medics and police helicopters. The men who shot him were now in hot pursuit. Sullimon looked in the rear view mirror. His pursuers were gaining on him. Sullimon could see the skyline of city lights far ahead of him. If he could reach the city in time he could easily lose them or at least have a better chance of someone calling the police. Sullimon thought for a second and then pressed the pedal to the floor. The red sports car darted forward at full speed and started to gain distance. The pursuers in the big cars also had nerves of steel to chase at such a high speed on a now wet road. They also saw the city lights ahead and wanted to stop the red sports car before it reached the city.

Robert Kirkland could not move his wounded leg. It felt numb. He felt bleeding from his back a few inches under his shoulder blade where a bullet had hit him. He was conscious and was still able to talk on his cell phone to the agent in charge and give a full report on what the meeting was all about. He sat motionless to conserve his energy. The pursuers increased the intensity of their firepower. Sullimon continued to return fire in short intervals to let the pursuers know that he still had ammunition.

Sullimon tried to encourage Kirkland, "Help is on the way."

Kirkland replied "Please listen to me. I am hurt. I am not going to make it. Let me out. I will stall them. At least one of us will make it."

"Sorry, my friend," Sullimon said, "I can not leave you. We will make it."

Some of the bullets hit the rear tires. The little sports car swerved all over the road as bullets ripped through its rear tires. The car came to a stop on the shoulder of the road. The pursuers from the luxury cars came out of their cars shooting. They shot the rear window. Bernard DeLoatch's motioned to two of his gangsters. They surrounded the car keeping out of the reach of the hand gun range. They riddled the sides of the car with machine gun bullets. Robert Kirkland died in the rain of bullets. Sullimon was hit bad but was not dead. He shot back a few times, but now his gun was empty. He heard the helicopters in the distance. He took out the flair gun and shot a flair in the air to give the helicopters their position. DeLoatch and his gangsters approached the little sports car and shot Sullimon at close range. Sullimon fell out of the car and tried vainly to attack one of the men, but before he could attack he was shot by machine gun.

Sheik Farooque came out of one of the luxury cars and moved quickly to retrieve the scrunched paper that he had given Robert Kirkland earlier. They quickly got into their cars and continued toward the city as police car sirens blared and helicopters passed by. Soon the luxury cars, which carried Bernard DeLoatch and Sheik Farooque, mingled with the city traffic.

By the time the agent in charge, police and the ambulances arrived, Robert Kirkland and Sullimon were dead.

Later on the Interpol chief got a call from the French coast guard that two of his employee who were supposed to stall Bernard DeLoatch were found on a rented fishing boat floating aimlessly, without any working communication equipment. They had been robbed of their wallets and cell phones and put on that boat. They were not harmed.

Roger Grace, Chief of Global Intelligence Services, was in his office sipping Bavarian coffee, without cream and sugar, as he always liked it. He was a hard-working man. He could always be found in his office, rain or shine, any time of the day or night. He was always clean cut, clean-shaven and immaculately dressed. His personal secretary, Ms. Jenni Bain, always saw him in his office no matter how early she arrived to work, or no matter how late she left. She always felt his presence behind the fortified, closed door of his office. She never saw him arriving or leaving. She had heard that Mr. Grace had an identical twin that filled in for him when he was out, or that he had an underground tunnel linking his residence to the office complex. Jenni Bain did not doubt the stories. She knew there were bunkers equipped with modern comforts and a maze of laboratories and electronic surveillance installations underneath the Global Intelligence Service complex.

A special telephone line for overseas contacts rang. It meant serious trouble overseas. Mr. Grace picked up the phone. It was the middle-eastern branch.

A male voice that did not exchange any pleasantries said, "Sir, Special Agent Robert Kirkland and his assistant, Sullimon, have been neutralized. A detailed report is being faxed to you."

Roger Grace stared into empty space. Wrinkles formed on his forehead because he remembered Robert Kirkland and Sullimon. They were two of his best agents. Anyone who eliminated them must be connected with someone powerful. "Do we have any suspects?" he asked.

"Everything is detailed in the report," the caller said, "We request assistance as soon as possible."

Roger Grace replied, "Help will be sent." He hung up the phone and the fax machine in his office started receiving the report. He looked at the report and his eyes widened with concern as he saw a familiar name, Bernard DeLoatch. He switched on the intercom and called his secretary, "Ms. Bain, have Mark Hunter report to my office immediately."

Miss Jennie Bain replied, "He is taking care of some personal business this week."

"Ms. Bain, I want him to drop every thing and report to my office immediately."

"Yes sir." Ms. Bain detected the concern in Mr. Grace's voice.

❦   ❦   ❦

Mark Hunter's lips entwined lovely Victoria Blake's lips. Hunter had met this health and fitness instructor on a group hike while vacationing in Maine. They were lying in front of a fireplace in a warm, beautifully decorated room of her apartment on a chilly night. Hunter's shirt and jacket and Victoria's pullover sweater were lying on the carpet. Two empty wineglasses were lying on a coffee table nearby.

"Oh, Mark," Victoria cooed, "I'm so glad I met you. I love your name, Mark Tracker Hunter." She clung tightly to his muscular body.

Mark Hunter returns, "The pleasure is all mine." He continued to kiss and embrace her beautiful body. He reached into his jacket and took out a box of condoms. He glanced at the lid of the box, which read "Be safe and live longer."

Suddenly a slow, beeping sound came from his cell phone. It meant that there was an emergency. Hunter looked at the repeatedly blinking message in green letters on the cell phone screen. It read, "Drop everything, and report immediately." Hunter pressed a three-numbers code on the cell phone, which meant that he had received the message.

Hunter sighed deeply and got up. Victoria stretched out her arms holding onto him. Hunter looked at Victoria's beautiful inviting body, and then gently dropped the box of condoms, which landed on lovely Victoria's belly, and started to dress.

Victoria sat up and sadly moaned, "Oh Mark, have I annoyed you?"

"No, my dear, you have been wonderful. It is something that I have to do."

Victoria got up, slid a nightgown on, and gave Hunter a passionate kiss. "Come back to me soon."

"You can count on that." Mark Hunter gently opened the door, got to his car and took off, while Victoria looked from the window.

Mark Hunter arrived at Roger Grace's office early in the morning. Jenni Bain sat behind her desk busy typing on her computer. Mark Hunter walked into the office and as usual offered Jenni Bain a box of chocolates. She looked at him adoringly. She took the chocolates and extended the other hand, which Mark Hunter gently held and kissed.

Jennie Bain remarked, "Mark, you don't look very happy. Did we interrupt you in the middle of something?" She smiled mischievously.

With all the mock, sad expression he could muster Mark Hunter said, "Miss Jenni Bain, you have no idea."

Jenni Bain smiled with satisfaction, but before she could say anything, Mr. Grace's voice sounded on her intercom. "Ms. Bain, would you please send Hunter in. We have no time to waste."

Turning to Hunter, Miss Jennie Bain said, "You better go in. He has been edgy." She smiled and threw a kiss. Mark Hunter opened the door and went into Grace's office, where Grace was sitting with Chief Donald Klein, from the Interpol office.

"Hunter, you know Mr. Klein, from the Interpol," Roger Grace said

"Yes sir."

Roger Grace, turning to Chief Donald Klein, "You know Mark T. Hunter. I am putting him in charge of this case."

"I've had the pleasure of briefly working with Mr. Mark Tracker Hunter in Vienna. I was most impressed. I think Mr. Hunter is the right man for the job."

"That brings us to the case at hand," Roger Grace says. He gave Hunter a manila folder, the same kind that Grace and Klein already had. "Hunter, I'm sorry to tell you that your friends, Robert Kirkland and Sullimon, were killed last evening while helping the Interpol. I'll let Mr. Klein explain what happened next."

Mr. Klein began, "The Interpol picked up the lead that Bernard DeLoatch was meeting with Sheik Farooque to discuss something very important. At my request Robert Kirkland agreed to impersonate Bernard DeLoatch, because as you know he resembled DeLoatch. So he went to meet with Sheik Farooque. The plan was that Robert Kirkland would meet with Sheik Farooque, and would find out the purpose of the meeting. My people were supposed to detain the real Bernard DeLoatch, and Robert Kirkland would get out of there before the real Bernard DeLoatch arrived to see Sheik Farooque. The Interpol had suspected that DeLoatch and Sheik Farooque were meeting about a sophisticated, illegal weapons and arms deal to some small country. They both deal with illegal weapons on the black market, and recently large quantities of sophisticated weapons have disappeared from many European countries supply depots without a trace. Everything was going well, until the people who were to stall DeLoatch failed and ended up in a boat without communication equipment. The real DeLoatch showed up at Sheik Farooque's place in the middle of the meeting with Kirkland. I am so sorry about what happened."

Mark Hunter replied, "I am so sorry to hear this news. Is Bernard DeLoatch roaming around free?"

"Yes," Roger Grace replied, "What Bernard DeLoatch and Sheik Farooque were discussing is extraordinary. They were talking about a legendary map that has the location of great treasures. Also, they talked about a small silver metal box that holds the pieces and contents of a strange box made out of strange substance and called the box of knowledge, along with a small diamond type crystal that powered that box. The most extraordinary thing is that it was given to a person by some strange beings that had great powers and could communicate through telepathy. These aliens were flying in a spaceship that could fly from one world to another. We could have ignored this whole story about aliens and flying spaceships, like some scientist have ignored the Roswell link to aliens but Mr. Klein received a call from another source." Mr. Grace motioned toward Donald Klein to speak. Donald Klein continued:

"The Interpol received a dispatch, of course, for a price we paid. This dispatch came from an employee of the reclusive billionaire, Michael Kavanaugh. The employee informed us that Bernard DeLoatch was hired by the billionaire to bring the contents of the broken pieces of the box of knowledge, along with the diamond crystal that powered the box, at any cost. The beginning fee was twenty million dollars, plus expenses, plus additional fees if things got complicated. We checked it out, according to the information we received, half of the money in the amount of ten million dollars from Michael Kavanaugh's account has already been transferred to a Swiss bank account that apparently belongs to Bernard DeLoatch."

Roger Grace interjected, "We have reason to believe that although Kavanaugh is a recluse and an eccentric, he is a shrewd businessman. He does not throw away twenty million dollars unless he was getting something worthwhile in return. My superiors, myself, Mr. Klein, and our science experts feel that this is worth exploring. It will also keep us on Bernard DeLoatch's tail, to bring him to justice."

Donald Klein apologized, "Mr. Grace, I have to leave. Mr. Hunter, all the Interpol resources and agents are there to assist you. Once again, I am very sorry about your friends' deaths." He excused himself and left.

Roger Grace spoke to Hunter, "Mark, are you familiar with the term, 'Hardening of the Microchips?'"

"Yes sir," Hunter replied, "The term is used about experimental research that is going on in private computer industries, world governments, and the whole Silicon Valley. Billions of dollars are being spent to develop a hardened silicon microchip. There has been little to no success."

"Excellent," an impressed Grace said, "Now do you know why so many resources and money is spent to create a hardened silicon microchip?"

"I believe our technology is based on an electronic, computerized communication and signaling system, which is transmitted and channeled through fragile silicon microchips. This could be rendered useless by the electromagnetic pulse or interference known as E.M.P., electromagnetic pulse. Any kind of thermonuclear explosion generates E.M.P., which could distort and disrupt the electronic communication. This could possibly bring civilization to a halt."

Roger Grace replied, "Do you know that there is a microchip somewhere on this planet made out of the hardest diamond-like substance? It is actually believed to be made by an alien society ... Many scientists think that if this crystal chip exists, there is a great wealth of advance knowledge and technology stored in this artifact. The few parchments that were bought by the museum show some mathematical and scientific computations, which are very advanced, even by present standards. That's why it cannot be ignored. Any country or group that controls the secrets of this alien technology will advance light years ahead of everyone else, and could control the whole planet. In the wrong hands the security of the whole-civilized world could be in danger."

Hunter agreed, "With this technology people like Kavanaugh could get rid of inferior competition and follow the twisted old dreams of world domination!"

"That's right," Grace said and continued, "Our sources have notified me that agents from every industrialized country—many other countries—have already sent agents in to find this technology…. You will be pitted against top agents from Russia, Germany—many countries—and don't forget Bernard DeLoatch and Kavanaugh." As he said this, the intercom communication button lit up and started to blink. "Yes, Ms. Bain?"

"Sir, Dr. Fraction is waiting for you in his lab."

"Thank you, Ms. Jenni Bain."

Grace pressed a button under his huge oak table and a bookcase that covered the wall on his right slid open. At the same time a red button blinked on Jenni Bain's desk. This meant that Grace should not be disturbed unless there was an extreme emergency.

Hunter followed Grace into a corridor through the trap door. At the end of the corridor was the door to Dr. Fraction's lab. Hunter had been to the lab before. On the right hand side of the door was a panel of buttons. Mr. Grace pressed the red, white and green buttons in unison and the door opened.

They walked into Dr. Fraction's lab. The lab had state of the art equipment; many chemical flasks and other scientific apparatus set up on lab tables. At the far end of the lab, a large area was left clear with the exception of a table. Thick fortified metallic walls surrounded the area around the table. Dr. Fraction was a slight built, serious looking man of medium height in a white lab coat.

"Hello meat man," Hunter joked.

Dr. Fraction, a little annoyed, said, "Hunter you are hardly funny. Please try to be serious. We have a lot of work to do. Hunter, give me your cell phone."

Hunter handed over his agency issued cell phone to Dr. Fraction, who put it in a drawer, and took out another that looked exactly like the other one. Dr. Fraction motioned Grace and Hunter to follow him. They walked toward the area where his assistants had set up a thick steel plate on the table in an upright position. Fraction continued his instructions, "Hunter, observe. If I press this knob where it says 'Clear' four times and then press the middle circular knob ..." Dr. Fraction pressed the circular knob as he held the cell phone like a gun pointing it toward a two-inch thick steel plate. An intense laser beam shot out of the cell phone and in seconds cut a hole through the steel plate.

"One more thing,"Dr. Fraction continued, "If you press the top of the phone it will transmit a homing signal which can be picked up by our agency and its branches all around the globe so your whereabouts will be known and help can arrive if you need it."

"Can I still make and receive phone calls?" Hunter asked sarcastically.

Ignoring the sarcasm Fraction said, "Yes. Your cell phone will perform all the functions of a conventional cell phone. The laser microchip apparatus is an additional function. It does not interfere with the normal functions of your cell phone."

"How clever of you,"Hunter said. He took the cell phone from Dr. Fraction and put it on his belt.

With a slight smile Fraction said, "I try."

"Glad to see you smile," Hunter replied, "I think there is hope for you yet."

"Thanks Hunter." Dr. Fraction reached into his desk drawer and took out a gold ring with a red stone and said, "Hunter, look at this little knob on the side of the ring. If you press this knob four times in quick sequence make sure to hold your breath for fifteen seconds because the knob will puncture a small-pressurized compartment under this red stone which is filled with a compressed and highly toxic colorless nerve gas which dissipates in fifteen seconds once activated. But in the first ten seconds it could render every living thing unconscious within an area of ten square feet. Its effect wears off within an hour."

Hunter asked, "Can the gas compartment be punctured after pressing it the first or the second time?"

"No," Fraction explained, "because the pointer on the knob will only be lined up to go through the hole of the gas compartment after it is pressed the fourth time." Fraction handed the ring to Hunter, who put it on his finger.

"Well meat man, you did it again," Hunter said with a mischievous grin, "For a second I thought there was a real gem in this ring."

Roger Grace thanked Dr. Fraction and he and Mark Hunter returned to Grace's office. Grace again pressed a button and the huge bookcase slid back to its place. He pressed another button and the red light on Jenni Bain's desk went off.

Roger Grace pressed the intercom button and said, "Ms. Jenni Bain, do we have the paperwork ready for Hunter?"

Jennie Bain walked into Grace's office with a large manila folder. "Everything you have asked for is here."

Roger Grace took the folder from Bain and gave it to Hunter. "Your passport, airplane tickets, contact people and other important information is included in this folder. Read through it. You are booked on a flight to Cairo. The ambassador, Jonathan Holland, and his staff will assist you and provide you with further details."

Mark Hunter walked out of Grace's office and saw Jenni Bain sitting at her desk. "Well Ms. Jenni Bain, I shall see you later, my dear."

Dramatically Jenni Bain said, "Hunter, be careful. Come and hold me before you go." Hunter embraced Jenni and she mockingly said, "I don't want to let you go."

Over the intercom Roger Grace exclaims, "Miss Jenni Bain, let him go!" They both grinned mischievously as Hunter left the office.

Michael Kavanaugh, the reclusive billionaire, sat in his study at the head of the huge conference table. He did not look happy. A very nervous, skinny man of medium height sat in a chair about five chairs away from Kavanaugh, looking through a thick file. Kavanaugh spoke to the jittery man, "Dean, we don't know how the Interpol got hold of the information that only you and a few other trusted administrators had access to."

Dean bleated, "I don't understand either, sir. The only explanation I can come up with is that by accident some one tapped into the file, got the information and told the Interpol."

Michael Kavanaugh pursed his lips to control his anger. "Do you know that once the Interpol gets information the whole world will know because the Interpol is an international organization? It makes me very unhappy. This kind of exposure I wanted to avoid at any cost, but I guess nothing is impossible. Maybe, as you say, someone did tap in by accident and informed the Interpol."

The nervous skinny man did not lift his eyes from the file, as if he tried to avoid looking at Kavanaugh. At that time the female receptionist voice sounded on the intercom, "Mr. Kavanaugh your appointment has arrived."

"Send him in," Kavanaugh replied, "I am sending the elevator down." Kavanaugh pressed a button out of countless buttons on a control panel to send the elevator down. After a few minutes the elevator door opened and the notorious Bernard DeLoatch walked in. Kavanaugh pointed toward the nervous, skinny man, and said "You have met with Mr. Dean. He was one of my confidential accountants who handled your transaction." Bernard DeLoatch nodded yes. Kavanaugh continued, "Dean, you can go back to your office, but keep me posted if you find out who leaked the information to the Interpol."

Dean, the jittery accountant, quickly said, "Thank you. I will keep you informed if anything comes up." He walked quickly to the elevator and was more than happy to get out of Kavanaugh's study. Kavanaugh pressed a button and the elevator door opened. Dean got into the elevator and waved nervously goodbye with his skinny hand as the elevator door closed.

Kavanaugh spoke to Bernard DeLoatch, "Are you positive that it was Dean who leaked the information to the Interpol?"

"Yes, we have positive ID. It was your accountant, Dean."

Kavanaugh nodded thoughtfully and pressed a button. A huge TV screen lit up on the front wall near the elevator. It showed Dean in the elevator. DeLoatch watched the screen and noticed a gaseous substance come out of tiny holes from the elevator walls Dean tried to pry open the elevator doors with his fingers. He choked and gagged as if desperately trying to breathe. The thick file had fallen from his hands.

Kavanaugh spoke in a loud unemotional voice, "Dean, you traitor. You are the one who leaked the information to the Interpol. You are going to pay for your treachery."

Bernard DeLoatch, himself a ruthless killer, was somewhat shocked and amazed at Kavanaugh's vengeful brutality. He saw Dean, who looked around like a frightened animal, as he continued to try to pry the door open with his fingers. After a few minutes Dean gave up the struggle and collapsed to the floor, dead.

Kavanaugh pressed a button and the elevator went to the basement. The elevator door opened and two hooded men entered, picked up all the papers from the floor, put them neatly back into the folder that Dean had carried, put Dean's body into a body bag, put the body bag onto the back of a pickup truck and left. The elevator door closed and the TV screen went dead.

Bernard DeLoatch said, "Well that was efficient, but now under these new developments there will be additional charges."

Kavanaugh replied, "As I have told you, money is no object. Just bring me the contents of the alien box of knowledge and the diamond crystal as soon as possible."

Bernard DeLoatch replied, "Consider it done." He went to the elevator to leave and hesitated a moment. Finally, he entered the elevator and left.

The KGB Chief sat in his office, going through a file. He had been awakened early in the morning by a special coded call from the Istanbul branch. The call and the report outlined detailed information that was received by the Interpol about the death of a top American secret agent and his associate.

The voice of his secretary shook him out of his deep thoughts, "Comrade Salisnakoff, Special Agent Nitasha Brincheska is reporting for assignment".

"Send her in," the KGB Chief replied. Nitasha, a ruthless agent, entered the office. She had fair skin, five-foot seven inches tall, light brown hair and striking hazel eyes. She was known as the scorpion of the Red Square.

The KGB chief addressed Nitasha, "We have reports that an alien technology, something like an extra-terrestrial computer with a diamond chip processor, exists. There is a map that shows the location of the remains of this technology."

Nitasha replied, "I have heard this legend. Thousands of years ago some extra terrestrial beings gave a little box of knowledge or a computer to an earthling in gratitude for his help. A diamond microchip processor powered the little computer-like box. It was supposed to be just a legend, but in real life a micro chip made out of the hardest substance, like a diamond, could revolutionize present day technology and put the country or entity who controls it light years ahead of everyone else."

The KGB chief grinned admiringly and said, "Comrade Nitasha, you have always met my expectations with the depth of your knowledge."

"Thank you, comrade."

The KGB chief continued, "It seems that this technology does exist because our sources have informed me that every country in the world has assigned their top agents to retrieve this artifact. I have alerted our Eastern Europe and Middle-Eastern branches that you are the agent that I am putting in charge of the operation. You will have absolute authority. Everyone else is to report to you and assist you as you command. We have booked your flight to Cairo. Your flight leaves in an hour. I have full confidence that you will bring this technology back for Russia. I am authorizing the triple 'O' code."

"The triple 'O' code," Nitasha replied, "Know objective, accomplish objective. If unable to accomplish, destroy objective target at any cost. I shall not disappoint you Comrade Salisnakoff."

Nitasha, scorpion of Red Square, left the KGB chief's office. Her name was earned because she was smart, but deadly.

❧   ❧   ❧

By the time Hunter's plane landed at the Cairo airport the hot middle-eastern sun was just beginning to bake the atmosphere. Ambassador Holland's trusted associate, Sharief, waited for Hunter at the airport. Hunter and Sharief had worked on many assignments and knew each other well. Hunter always found Sharief a competent and trust-worthy person. Sharief had once, on another assignment, almost scarified his life to save Hunter's life.

Sharief, helped Hunter with his luggage. Hunter noticed as he was gathering his luggage, that other eyes were interested in his arrival. Hunter noticed a European man, of medium height and well built who seemed to pretend to be a tourist. The "tourist" was nonchalantly looking around as if trying to find someone. In the heat, the tourist tugged at his shirt collar, but was actually taking a picture of Hunter with a hidden camera. The tourist left the airport alone.

Another, noticing Hunter's arrival, was a young newspaper salesman dressed in clothes that a typical newsman could not afford. When Hunter and Sharief headed toward the exit doors the salesman threw his newspapers pile in a waste receptacle and disappeared.

Hunter said to Sharief, "People like taking pictures with hidden cameras."

Sharief smiled and said, "Why is it every time you are here people like to take your picture?"

"Perhaps they like me," Hunter smiled.

Sharief drove an unmarked car, no official embassy seals or signs on it. He and Hunter got into the car and headed toward the embassy. While driving, Hunter and Sharief noticed a green jeep with tinted glass windows slowly following them in traffic. Hunter could make out three passengers, two European males and a European female. After a few miles the green jeep took a turn and mingled with the traffic going the opposite direction. Sharief seemed puzzled. Was the green jeep following them, and if so why did it turn around?

Now they were on an open, less traveled road. Hunter said, "My dear friend Sharief, the deadly scorpion of Red Square, Ms. Nitasha Brincheska just let us know that she is in the area. She was in that green jeep."

Sharief nodded and said that things were going to get hot. No sooner had Sharief finished his sentence, then a big luxury car darted toward them. This was the car driven by Bernard DeLoatch's henchmen. Sharief skillfully drove the car as a barrage of bullets came from the luxury car.

Hunter took out his cell phone, pressed a button, and an intense laser beam shot out hitting the front end of the luxury car. It burnt a hole right through the motor. The luxury car went out of control and burst into flames.

❦   ❦   ❦

When they got to the embassy gate the guards at the checkpoint looked at Sharief's car suspiciously, but when they saw Sharief wave at them, they opened the gate and asked what happened. Sharief replied, "A little accident.".

At the embassy Mr. Holland asked in a concerned manner, "Are you two all right? What happened?"

Hunter replied, "Somehow news of my arrival leaked out."

Surprised Mr. Holland said, "That is impossible. Only Ms. Taylor, Sharief and I knew of your arrival. We have always shared information of a sensitive nature."

Pondering, Hunter said, "It is not about you three. It's something else, something unusual. Have you had your phones fixed recently or saw someone on a nearby telephone pole fixing the lines?"

Ms. Taylor, the ambassador's executive secretary, remembered that someone did come in to fix the phone line. "They had been working fine," she said, "But two days ago I received a call from the regional telephone company that they had gotten a complaint from our office that some phone lines were not working and they were sending the technicians out to take care of the problem. I thought maybe someone from our office had experienced a problem with their telephone and had called the company. I did not pay any attention at the time. Two technicians came in and worked on our phone lines."

Ms. Taylor picked up the daily activity logbook. It showed that two days ago someone had worked on the office phone lines. The signatures were so ineligible that it could not be read. Ms. Taylor called the regional telephone company. The company's customer services administrator told her that they did not receive any complaint from the embassy and did not send any one out.

Ms. Taylor then said, "One of our guards, Corporal Stevenson, signed them in and watched them. He's been with us for twelve years, quite reliable. He is on duty now."

Ambassador Holland turned to Sharief and asked him to call the gate number where Stevenson worked and ask him to step in for a minute. Before Sharief could make the call, Hunter told them to not bother. "He does not know any-thing," Hunter said and then said to Ms Taylor, "You were in and out of the office. Can you recall what phone lines these so-called technicians were working on? We should check all the phones but we should start with what they had worked on."

Ms. Taylor replied, "It was mostly in the main office area where we are now."

"May I take a look at these telephones?" Hunter asked the Ambassador. The Ambassador told him to go ahead and Hunter took the receiver apart, pulling out a small, flat metallic object, "Here is your leak," he said.

Hunter and Shareif checked all the telephones in the area and took out the same kind of metallic listening devices from the phones that were in the main office and the lobby area, but were not found in the telephones found in other areas.

Mr. Holland told Ms. Taylor and Sharief that everything should be checked and double-checked. He told them that whenever outsiders enter the grounds for repairs, drop off deliveries, or pick up items they should be positively identified—who they were and who sent for them.

Ms. Tayler and Sharief nodded their heads and said "Yes, Mr. Holland." Ms. Taylor added, "In the next ten minutes I will be sending out an all staff emergency memo, stating your orders about embassy security, effective immediately."

"Thank you," Mr. Holland said and turned to Hunter and Sharief. "I have invited the Commissioner of Police. He is a good friend of mine. He will take you both to see Professor Youseff Shameil, who is an authority on ancient scrolls and artifacts. You need to know the Police Commissioner in case you face any problem with the local police during your investigation."

❦   ❦   ❦

The Commissioner of Police arrived in plain clothes. Mr. Holland introduced Hunter and Sharief, "I want you two to meet Police Commissioner, Rasheed Shamus, a good friend of mine." Hunter and Sharief shook hands with the Police Commissioner, a bright and friendly person. The Police Commissioner told them that he came in plain clothes and an unmarked police car so that when they went to meet with Professor Youseff Shameil it would not attract attention.

On the way to see Professor Youseff Shameil the Commissioner of Police told them that the Professor worked as a translator and evaluator of ancient languages and artifacts at the museum where the recently discovered parchments were brought in.

Professor Youseff was expecting them. He was a short, light built man in his late fifties and wore thick glasses. He greeted the Commissioner of Police, "Nice to see you Commissioner."

"It is nice to see you also, Professor.… These are my friends I told you about. See if you can help them."

"Your friends are very welcome. I will do everything I can to help them." The professor then asked Hunter and Sharief, "What can I do for you, gentlemen?"

Hunter replied, "We are interested in the ancient parchments that you translated a few days ago. Please tell us the details about the legend described in those parchments." Hunter was glad that the Commissioner of Police knew the professor personally because the professor may not have wanted to divulge any information in detail if not for the Commissioner's recommendation

The professor's wife brought in some refreshments, and the Commissioner of Police, along with Hunter and Sharief, thanked her and the professor.

"You are most welcome," the Professor said. "With all the help I receive from the Commissioner for my museum work, that's the least I can do for you gentlemen. Now getting back to the parchments. The parchments that were brought to me were authentic; thousands of years old. They contain writings about an old legend.

"About 300 BC a man by the name of Eliezer Abishu, a well respected leader of his community, helped two alien beings, whose space ship, as they told him, developed some mechanical problems and crashed on the planet Earth. They were hurt and needed help. They communicated with him through telepathy. Eliezer, instead of running away from them and causing problems for them treated them with kindness and helped them. He shared with them his most valuable possession: a diamond necklace. The aliens were able to use the diamonds to restore the ship's energy packs.

"They liked Eliezer very much and before they left they gave him a little box of knowledge. It was like a computer with extraterrestrial knowledge. This computer was powered by a microchip that was made by a diamond or diamond-like hard substance from another planet. Later on it got broken into pieces in an accident. But the microchip that was made of diamond or a diamond-like substance did not get destroyed. Eliezer took the broken pieces and the micro-chip processor made of diamond crystal and put them in a silver box hoping that some day his off-spring would have the knowledge to fix it or with some miracle the aliens would come back and help fix the box of knowledge.

"Generation after generation passed by and their land got invaded and conquered. The offspring of Eliezer hid the silver container that held the broken pieces of the alien computer and the diamond microchip, along with other large treasures that the aliens had given them. The offspring made a map of the location where everything was hidden."

The professor paused and asked them if they had any questions so far.

Hunter said that he had a question. "Was there a map in those parchments that you translated?"

"No, and another strange thing happened. The parchments that we are talking about were stolen from the museum. Confidentially, I and some of my associates, think that the map might be with Zahir Jamal, the owner of the Sand Rock Café. He is the cousin of Sheik Farooque, who is believed to be the person who had stolen all the parchments from the desert. They both do business together. But be very careful they are very dangerous men."

Hunter and Sharief thanked the professor and the Commissioner and returned to the embassy.

❦   ❦   ❦

At the embassy there was a special message from Hunter's boss, Roger Grace. The message had been dropped off through a confidential courier. The message read that Zahir Jamal, the owner of the Sand Rock Café, was expecting Hunter. It was urgent that they meet immediately. Zahir Jamal was trying to find appropriate buyers to bid on an ancient map. He had the map that everyone was looking for. The message further read that the treasury department had authorized Hunter to obtain the map at any cost.

Hunter told Sharief and Ambassador Holland, "The professor was right in his assumption that Zahir Jamal had the map."

Hunter and Sharief immediately left for the Sand Rock Café. It was a cozy little café with a well-to-do clientele. Since it was after the afternoon dinner rush, customers were few. Some people were still sitting in their favorite spots. The bar area was tastefully separated from the dining area.

Hunter said to the Matron D., "My name is Mark Hunter. This is my associate, Sharief. Mr. Zahir Jamal is expecting me."

The Matron D. cautiously looked at them and replied, "I shall let him know that you are here." She made a call with her cell phone and told Hunter, "Mr. Zahir Jamal has an appointment right now, but he can see you after the appointment." She gave them hospitality cards, "In the meantime, please use these and enjoy our hospitality."

Hunter and Sharief went to the bar. They showed the cards to the muscle bound bartender, who was not only tending bar, but also keeping an eye on Zahir Jamal's office not far away. Hunter's professional eyes noticed that he was armed. He thought that the bartender probably also worked as a bodyguard. Hunter saw a few other well-built and well-dressed middle-eastern men, who mingled with customers, but also hung around in the vicinity of Zahir Jamal's office. They probably served as body guards also.

Hunter ordered a Bourbon and Sharief ordered beer. They picked up their drinks and sat down at a little table near Jamal's office to wait for the meeting.

The office was about twenty-five feet away. On the door a sign read, "Zahir Jamal, Manager". Hunter and Sharief saw two men walk toward the office. One was a short middle-eastern man Hunter had seen in a picture. He was Sheik Farooque, and the other one was a well-built, big European man that every secret agent knew was the ruthless and notorious Bernard DeLoatch.

As they neared the door of the office, a medium-height, medium-weight man opened the door and let them in. The man was Zahir Jamal.

Inside the office, Bernard DeLoatch spoke in an annoyed manner, "Sheik Farooque and Jamal, I thought we had an agreement that no one would know that you have the map and that I was going to buy it from you—unless I didn't pay the price you asked—but now my sources tell me that you are putting this on an open market for anyone to bid."

Sheik Farooque tried to calm Bernard DeLoatch and said, "Mr. DeLoatch, my cousin Jamal did not understand our deal. I apologize for that."

"I have the one million American dollars that we agreed upon, in cash, in my brief case, right here, to buy the map," DeLoatch replied coldly and calmly, "It is as simple as, 'I give you the money, you give me the map', and we go our ways." DeLoatch opened the briefcase he was carrying and showed them the money. "You can count it if you like."

Sheik Farooque looked at the money greedily. Zahir Jamal spoke with a cunning smile, "Gentlemen, we have a new development. We have an American, a Russian, a French and a German buyer—all who want to bid for this map."

Sheik Farooque did not like to go back on his deals, "But Jamal, we gave Bernard our word."

"Farooque, that was in the old days and times. Now-a-days, one's word is not even worth a camel dropping in the desert sand."

Sheik Farooque protested but Bernard DeLoatch said curtly, "All right. I'll bid with the others." Zahir Jamal winked and smiled a winning smile at his cousin. Bernard DeLoatch had a thin smile on his lips, with his teeth showing, like a wolf ready to sink his teeth into his prey's neck. "But," Bernard continued with a ruthless grin, "Before you raise the price, I would like to see the map just to make sure that I am bidding on an authentic artifact and not just wasting my time."

"That is impossible," Zahir Jamal replied with an air of attitude, "The map remains in the safe." He patted a large built-in safe in the wall. "It remains in the safe until the transaction is complete and the full amount is deposited in our Swiss account. If any party does not like the terms they can leave." Sheik Farooque watched his cousin with a mixed feeling of admiration and caution. He knew that nobody dared double-cross Bernard DeLoatch, but he liked the way his cousin was making the great Bernard DeLoatch sweat. Zahir Jamal was very happy with himself. He basked in the glory of how he handled Bernard DeLoatch.

Both Sheik Farooque and his cousin Zahir Jamal were so pleased with the idea that they were going to make a lot of money that they did not pay attention to the changes in Bernard DeLoatch's expression and hand movements. They did not notice the ruthless grin on Bernard DeLoatch's face when Zahir Jamal had pointed out that the authentic map was in the safe in the wall, no more then ten feet in front of him. It was Sheik Farooque who looked in disbelief as he noticed the gun with the silencer in Bernard DeLoatch's hand. By the time Sheik Farooque overcame his shock and reality set in, and before he could warn Zahir Jamal, who was still oblivious to his surroundings, rubbing the safe with a dust cloth, it was too late. With a popping sound, no louder than the opening of a champagne bottle, a bullet ejected from the gun and hit Sheik Farooque in the forehead instantly freezing all his activities as the bullet ripped through his brain. Sheik Farooque's dead body slumped in the chair.

By the time Zahir Jamal turned around and realized the situation, Bernard DeLoatch had moved quickly toward him and put his big hand on Jamal's mouth, lifting his flailing body like a rag doll, and whispered, "Open the safe."

Zahir Jamal nodded his head in compliance. Bernard DeLoatch let one of Jamal's hands go free. Zahir Jamal moved his free hand toward the safe to open it, but with a quick, agile motion he moved toward a red button, which was an alarm. Bernard DeLoatch quickly pulled Jamal back before his hand could touch the alarm. Zahir Jamal's eyes widened with fear as Bernard DeLoatch crushed his neck. DeLoatch let the limp body gently drop to the floor, and as it did one of Jamal's spread arms hit a thin alarm wire on the floor.

Bernard DeLoatch reached toward the safe but the alarms went off. He cursed under his breath. He heard the sound of many footsteps running toward the office door. There was loud banging on the door. Somebody outside yelled, "Get the master key, Habbib! It is in the register."

Bernard DeLoatch quickly took out a fake mustache, with a miniature device attached to it, that fitted snugly into his nostrils. He also took out a pair of goggles and put them on. They fitted snugly around his snake-like, shiny eyes. Somebody turned the key in the lock. Bernard DeLoatch took out two gray spheres the size a golf ball from his pocket. As the door opened he hid behind the door. As people poured into the office he hurled those spheres onto the floor. Instantly the room filled with thick, white, toxic smoke. DeLoatch timed it precisely so that nobody saw him. The employees, the lookouts and bodyguards for Zahir Jamal, who entered the office were blinded. They coughed and choked as they pushed and shoved each other to get out of the office. Bernard DeLoatch, who was not affected by the toxic smoke, easily blended in with the group of coughing and choking people and walked out of the room unnoticed.

Police officers and ambulances arrived, and moved the crowd of people away from the office. The detectives tried to talk to the employees and customers to collect information. Bernard DeLoatch walked by Hunter, who calmly sipped his drink. Hunter recognized DeLoatch in his disguise, and followed him as DeLoatch walked out of the Café. A big car pulled up and Hunter jotted down the license plate number. Bernard DeLoatch got in the car and sped away.

❖   ❖   ❖

Hunter told Sharief to go back to the embassy and wait for him, while he planned to contact the Police Commissioner. Hunter walked across the street to the Café La Breese and called the Commissioner of Police asking him if he could go over to the Sand Rock Café with him to investigate what happened and to check out Zahir Jamal's office. Hunter kept a close watch on the café from across the street while he waited for the Commissioner. While he waited a big car stopped near the Café La Breese and a beautiful woman with a big straw hat got out of the car with a young, muscular man. They both walked toward a door adjacent to the Café that led to an upstairs apartment. The woman stopped for a fraction of a second and surveyed the surrounding, her striking hazel eyes looked at Hunter as she continued on her way, opened the apartment lock and went in. Hunter recognized her as the beautiful and ruthless Russian agent, Nitasha Brincheska. This made two things clear in Hunter's mind. One, the reason he did not see her in the Sand Rock Café was because she was able to watch every thing from the apartment across the street. Two, no one had gotten the alien map or knew the whereabouts of the map because otherwise the scorpion of Red Square would not still be there. Hunter surmised that the map and the information about the whereabouts of the alien artifacts were still locked away somewhere in Zahir Jamal's office.

The Commissioner of Police met Hunter at the Café La Breese and said, "Sheik Farooque and Zahir Jamal are dead. I am going to see the bodies and then permit the ambulance to take them to the city morgue." He handed Hunter an identification pass and told him to put it on his jacket and follow him closely as they walked toward the café.

The police and employees of the Sand Rock Café were the only ones still left there to complete the questioning and gather information. Officers guarded The Sand Rock Café doors. They saluted the Commissioner and opened the doors. Homicide squad members also saluted the Commissioner as he approached them. The Commissioner said to one of the officers in charge, "Captain Rahman, show us where the bodies were found."

Captain Rahman led them to Zahir Jamal's office. The captain turned around and walked back to the entrance door. Hunter watched the captain walk out the office and saw him talk to Nitasha, who was waiting at the entrance door with the muscular European man he had seen earlier. The captain let Nitasha and the man into the Café and gave passes to them.

Hunter knew right away that he had to move fast and search fast. He had to find whatever he could find in Zahir Jamal's office, which would help him to locate the map and the alien artifacts. Quickly, Hunter thoroughly examined the office. The safe was untouched. Bernard DeLoatch had not been able to open it. Hunter examined Zahir Jamal's body. He removed a square locket that had been tied to his upper arm near the armpit with a black string. No one noticed Hunter removing the locket. The Commissioner of police was busy examining Sheik Farooque's body. Hunter moved toward the safe.

Captain Rahman stormed in, confronted the Commissioner of Police, and pointed at Mark Hunter, "What is he doing here? He should not be here?"

"This man is with me," the Commissioner said, "He is kind of a specialist in these matters. I brought him along to give us a hand."

"But sir," Captain Rahman protested, "I don't want anyone to interfere with the evidence. We are capable of handling it."

"I am fully aware of your capabilities, Captain. Now let me finish my work and do not interrupt me. Is that clear?"

"Yes, Sir," Captain Rahman grumbled.

In the mean time the forensic lab technicians arrived and started lifting fingerprints. After collecting a few objects from the office for evidence the lab crew left. As soon as the lab crew left, the Police Commissioner told Captain Rahman, "You can have the bodies removed and taken to the morgue, and inform their families."

"Right away, Sir."

The Commissioner asked Hunter, "Are you finished?"

"Yes, I am done. Could you drop me off at the embassy? And thank you for the help."

"It is my pleasure." They both walked out of Zahir Jamal's office. Hunter looked around. There was no sign of Nitasha Brincheska. The ambulance crew removed the bodies from the office and left. Hunter and the Commissioner of Police walked toward the exit doors when they saw Captain Rahman. Captain Rahman told the Commissioner that he would post two officers around the clock to guard the place until the investigation was complete.

"Very good, Rahman. I know I can count on you."

"Thank you, sir."

Hunter saw that the Commissioner's comment made Captain Rahman very happy.

The Sand Rock Café was empty accept for a few officers. Captain Rahman locked Zahir Jamal's office and walked to the exit door with other officers. After locking the main entrance door he told two of the officers that they were on duty. Before leaving he told them that they should not leave until their replacement arrived and everything was secure. They were to let him know immediately if there was any problem.

❦   ❦   ❦

Hunter and the Police Commissioner went to the Commissioner's car. As they drove to the embassy Hunter asked, "Is Captain Rahman a trustworthy person?"

"Rahman is basically a good man but does not like people from outside the department interfering." Hunter did not tell the Commissioner that the captain only questioned his presence in Jamal's office after talking to a Russian agent.

The Commissioner dropped Hunter off at the embassy and said, "Hunter, if you need me, do not hesitate to get in touch with me."

"Thank you, Commissioner. I will do that."

Sharief was waiting for Hunter at the embassy. When Hunter entered the embassy Sharief followed him to his room and closed the door. Hunter took out the locket that he had removed from Zahir Jamal's body. He showed it to Sharief.

Sharief looked at the square metal piece and said, "This is called 'The Taveez'. Many people wear it to keep them from sickness and other evils. There's usually a prayer written on a paper; then the folded paper is put in the metallic casing which is called 'The Taveez.'"

Sharief pressed a little knob on the locket. The locket opened up and Sharief took out a neatly folded paper. On the paper there were six numbers written in the Arabic language. Sharief translated the numbers, 85-73-62. Sharief said, "It looks like a combination number for a locker, but where?"

"The answer might be in the safe at the Sand Rock Café," Hunter replied, "We have to get into the Café."

"We can ask the Commissioner," Sharief suggested.

"I don't know if he'll go for that, and even if did, he might have to get it cleared and I don't want too many people to know about this."

"Then how do we get in when everything is locked up and under police surveillance?" Sharief asked.

"I think I have an idea. Maybe the Commissioner could help us, indirectly, but we need to go through Ambassador Holland."

Hunter called Ambassador Holland, and he and Sharief went to the ambassador's office. Hunter told the ambassador that he needed to enter Zahir Jamal's office in the Sand Rock Café because the answer to finding the map and the alien artifact was in that office.

"We could ask the Police Commissioner to take care of it," suggested the ambassador.

"That's what we wanted to talk to you about. Maybe the Commissioner could indirectly help us because there are agents from many different countries who are working on this." Hunter also mentioned how Captain Rahman helped the KGB secret agent, Nitasha Brincheska. "If we bring in the Commissioner of Police to openly and directly help us, they might bring in someone higher then him.

"Sharief and I have to get in without any one seeing us. It can not wait. We need a big wooden box that I can sit in. We have to drill holes in it so I will be able to breathe while I am in it. It should be delivered to the Sand Rock Café as bulk oil and spices supplies that need to be delivered and put in the stock room. Sharief will put the box on a handcart and take it to the stock room. It is not very bright in the café in the nighttime, so Sharief will stay hidden in the stock room, until we are ready to search the office. That's where we could use the Commissioner's help to persuade the officers to let Sharief bring the delivery in."

Ambassador Holland smiled admiringly and said, "Very good gentlemen. Sharief will drive the delivery truck to the Café. We will have the Commissioner of Police there to tell the officers on duty to let the delivery in. Have one of the embassy guards go with you, but stay hidden in the truck. When Sharief is safely inside the cafe with the big delivery box with Hunter in it, the embassy guard will wait for five minutes and then very quietly and carefully slip in the driver seat and drive the delivery truck away.

"We have big, empty, wooden boxes that we use for shipping our materials. I think they are big enough to accommodate Hunter." He called one of the embassy guards to inform him that he would be working with Hunter and Sharief. The ambassador called the Commissioner of Police and asked him to come over, urgent.

By the time the Commissioner arrived, Hunter and Sharief had the wooden box ready. A banner-sized label for the box was made which read, "Exotic Oils and Spices". The ambassador told the Commissioner of Police about the plan. He also told him about Captain Rahman's friendship with the ruthless, Russian agent. The Police Commissioner said, "I knew something was not right. Captain Rahman had been acting strange. I am glad that you did not explain your plan on the phone because Rahman was keeping an eye on my movements." He spoke to Sharief and Hunter, "Well gentlemen, I am heading toward Sand Rock Café. I will see you there."

❦   ❦   ❦

It was dark when the delivery truck carrying a big, wooden box stopped in front of the Sand Rock Café and backed toward the entrance doors. Sharief lowered the box with a tailgate lift, took out a hand jack and was removing the crate when the officers on duty came over and yelled, "Hey! You can not bring that box in here!"

"Look officers. I am just the delivery man," Sharief explained, "I was told to bring these supplies over here and put them in the stock room. I got children to feed. I don't make delivery, I don't get paid. I did not know there was a problem here."

At that time the commissioner reached the officers. He had parked his car a few blocks from the Sand Rock Café, and walked to the Café. He said to the officers, "What is going on? What seems to be the problem?"

The officers on duty saluted the Commissioner of Police and one of the officers pointed toward Sharief, "This man wants to take a crate of supplies inside the café in the stockroom."

Sharief repeated to the Commissioner, "Sir, I make my living making deliveries. If I don't deliver I don't get paid."

"Let the guy put the supplies in," the Commissioner told the officers.

One of the officers opened the door, and the other gave Sharief a hand with the box to get it in. The officer and Sharief were so busy with the box they did not notice that the Commissioner had gone into the building. The Commissioner walked into the building and moved quickly, hiding in the restroom, which was half way down the corridor before the stockroom. The stockroom was at the end of the corridor. Once the box was inside Sharief thanked the officer and told him that he didn't need any more help; he could finish taking it to the stock room himself.

When Sharief got to the stockroom door, the Commissioner caught up with him. He helped Sharief move the box inside the unlocked stock room and closed the door. They helped Hunter out of the box. Hunter was surprised to see the Commissioner, who whispered, "I decided to join you guys. Maybe I will learn something".

"It will be a pleasure to have you with us," Hunter quietly replied.

Inside the café only some night-lights provided a small glow of light. Hunter and Sharief heard the delivery truck start and leave. The officers on guard did not even notice that the delivery man had never left the building. Hunter and Sharief wore black clothing. Hunter took out two masks from his little duffel bag, put one on and gave the second one to Sharief, who also put on the mask.

One of the officers guarding the entrance door asked his partner, "Where did the Commissioner go?"

"He probably left while we were helping the delivery guy," the other officer replied.

*   *   *

Meanwhile a pair of trained and experienced eyes watched everything from a second story apartment window across the street. The KGB Agent, Nitasha Brincheska, the scorpion of Red Square, paced back and forth in the apartment. A high-powered binocular and other surveillance equipment was set up in the apartment. She and her driver, André, were both dressed in tight black clothing. They were waiting for Captain Rahman, who had promised the Russian agent to help her get into the Sand Rock Café. She noticed the delivery being made and she made a comment that the crate was large enough to hold a grown man.

Her driver, who did not seem to be very bright, chimed in, "Maybe they ordered a lot of supplies."

Nitasha Brincheska said in an annoyed manner, "The café is closed. Nobody makes deliveries in the night time, especially when there are no employees."

She also noticed that the Police Commissioner had entered the building, but did not come out. She smiled amusingly and thought to herself that it could possibly be Hunter in that big crate as a way to get into the café. "Very clever," she thought, "And the Commissioner is helping him." She made a mental note that Captain Rahman should not know about this; otherwise Rahman might hesitate to get involved with helping her. She was glad that André did not notice the Commissioner of Police; otherwise he might mention it to Captain Rahman. André was busy sneaking peaks at Nitasha's well-proportioned breasts.

❦   ❦   ❦

Inside the stock room Hunter suggested to the Commissioner that if anything went wrong the Commissioner should identify himself and pretend that he, himself was doing undercover surveillance.

Hunter and Sharief gently opened the door of the stockroom and crawled toward Zahir Jamal's office, which was not far away. The Commissioner had wanted to accompany Hunter and Sharief but he felt he was too out of shape for that kind of excursion, so instead he very carefully followed by walking behind Hunter and Sharief, who had reached the office and had already opened the door lock. All three entered the office.

Hunter walked toward the safe and took out his cell phone. He pressed the combination to change it into a laser, pointed it toward the lock on the safe and pressed a button. With a low, humming sound an intense laser beam shot out and cut a hole through the half-inch thick steel door. Hunter pressed a button and the humming stopped. The Police Commissioner reached out and touched the cell phone. It was not even warm or hot. He was impressed.

Sharief opened the safe. It contained a few bundles of local currency, a semi-automatic loaded handgun, and an accounting register. Hunter and his friends could not find anything that even closely resembled a map. Hunter moved his hand gently on the side of the walls and felt a little bump on the right side of the wall. He pressed the bump and a little compartment opened. Inside the compartment was a key. There was a three-digit number on the key, 219. Sharief looked at the key and whispered, "I know these kind of keys are used for a downtown train station rental locker."

They heard the new shift of officers arriving and the other officers leave. They heard footsteps coming toward the office. The Police Commissioner whispered in anger, "These officers are supposed to guard the entrance, not come into the building!"

Hunter grinned and whispered, "Who says these are your officers?"

The Commissioner looked at Hunter and said, "Oh." He understood that Hunter was insinuating that these people could be impostors.

Everything went dark. Someone had blown a fuse. The Police Commissioner noticed the resourcefulness of the people who were trying to get the map. The local law authorities could not stop them, just as Hunter had told him.

Sharief took out a pencil flashlight. They hid behind two big cabinets, which were against the wall on the opposite side of the safe. Then Sharief quickly turned off the light.

While feeling their way in the dark Hunter's hand felt a loose brick on the wall.

The office door gently opened. Hunter could see two shadowy figures, a big male and a short, stocky figure that had entered the office. The short man flashed a thin flashlight at the safe, and raced toward it.

He looked at the safe and said angrily, "Someone has already been here."

The big man said, "Henrick, this safe has a secret compartment on the side wall. Zahir Jamal's cousin told me that. Check that, also."

Henrick replied in anger, "The secret compartment is empty, also."

The tall man said, "Let me take a look at it." He moved closer to the safe and flashed the flashlight thoroughly inside the safe, and said, "Whatever was in there is gone. I don't like this. Let us get out of here."

Henrick whispered profanities and spoke to the big man, "DeLoatch, why the hell you killed Zahir Jamal without getting the map or at least finding out everything?"

The big man snapped back, "He told me that the map was in the safe, and he also told me that he was going to sell it to the Americans or Russians. I saw the American agent in the Café waiting for him. We will get it back from whoever got it. Let's go."

Henrick's cell phone began to ring. "What's going on?" he said.

A male voice told him that three Russian agents were entering the Café.

Captain Rahman had ordered the guards to check out the rear of the building, while he would wait in the front till they finished their round. That had given the Russian agent, Nitasha and her assistants, time to slip into the café.

Henrick replied, "We are getting out. There is nothing here. Someone was here before us."

Before Henrick could put the cell phone in his pocket the caller said in a panicked tone, "Lee Sung and his agents just killed Dietrick! I think they used a poison dart!"

Henrick ordered the caller, "Get out of there!" He spoke to the person with him,"DeLoatch, I have strict orders from my government to pull out of the deal if I feel that it is not worth it. I think it is not worth it, especially when the Americans and Russian are involved and one of them has the upper hand. We do not want to start an espionage conflict with these superpowers."

DeLoatch did not answer.

Henrick and DeLoatch moved quickly and disappeared in the dark.

Henrick whispered quietly to DeLoatch, "I have already lost one of my best agents, Dietrick. Dietrick could handle ten men with his bare hands, but he could not fight a poison dart in the dark".

Henrick and DeLoatch saw that the stockroom door was open. They entered, leaving the door ajar. They could see three shadowy figures moving slowly toward the office. When the three shadowy figures went into the office, Henrick and DeLoatch came out of the stockroom and left the Café. There were no guards at the Café doors.

When the three entered the office, one of the newcomers touched the safe door. It was a woman's voice that whispered, "It is open. Somebody's been here. Be careful."

Hunter, who was still hiding in the office, could recognize that voice anywhere. He had heard it on tapes for enemy agents to be aware of, as well as confronting her on many missions. It was Agent Nitasha Brincheska, with two other agents.

Many footsteps were heard coming toward the office. Nitasha whispered to her assistants, "Do not shoot unless it is necessary. Hide!" As luck would have it, she went behind the cabinets where Hunter and his friends were hiding. She was right next to Hunter, but showed no surprise, as if she expected him to be there. She whispered, "I hope the wooden box was comfortable."

Hunter smiled and replied, "I have had better transportation." He gestured to Nitasha to have more room and be comfortable. Nitasha bowed her head in mock thankful courtesy.

Her assistants had hid behind the office door. Someone gently pushed open the door. One of Nitasha's assistants opened fire, but no one was hit. Nitasha grumbled angrily under her breath, "Idiots, they are going to get killed!"

One of the Russian agents poked his head out a little to better see who had opened the door. A poison dart caught him in the throat. He sagged with a scream.

For a while there was complete silence; then two slim figures in ninja clothing crawled in through the door. The second Russian agent opened fire on them. One of the people, who were crawling, screamed and lay still. The taller figure threw a metal star, which hit the Russian agent in the forehead, and he fell to the ground. Nitasha took aim through the space between the two cabinets and shot the other ninja, who groaned and laid still.

The Commissioner slowly moved out of his hiding place to check the room. Hunter quickly pulled him back, just in time before a poisonous metal star came flying toward him. It hit the wall right where the Police Commissioner would have been, if not for Hunter.

Nitasha, again took aim through the space between the cabinets, and shot the ninja. The figure screamed and stopped moving. Hunter felt around the top of the cabinet and found some account registers. He threw them at the figure but no movement came. Flashing police cruiser lights and sirens surrounded the building. The lights returned inside the Café. Nitasha, with gun drawn, carefully came out of hiding and checked the ninja. He was dead. She checked her two assistants. They also were dead.

In the mean time, Hunter took out the key that he had taken out from the secret compartment of the safe and quickly removed the loose brick from the wall and hid the key in the opening. He carefully placed the brick back in the wall. Hunter, Sharief and the Commissioner came out from behind the cabinets.

Captain Rahman came into the building with a lot of policemen. Nitasha left the office and talked to Captain Rahman. The Commissioner, Sharief and Hunter came out of the office and met the captain in the hallway. The captain and the other officers saluted the Commissioner. Captain Rahman said to the Commissioner that he had to search Hunter and Sharief and that he had already searched Nitasha Brincheska.

The Commissioner said, "Captain, there are some dead bodies in the office. Call the lab technicians and homicide detectives."

The Captain told two officers to search Hunter and Sharief. Hunter winked at Nitasha and asked the captain, "What are we looking for?"

The captain spoke arrogantly, "Something that you might have stolen from the office safe!"

Hunter lifted his hands and said,"Search me."

Two of the officers searched Hunter thoroughly and took out his gun, cell phone, and a few other objects, but found nothing of importance. While the officers had been searching Hunter, Nitasha slipped into the office and then came out. The officers gave Hunter his belongings back. Captain Rahman told Nitasha, Hunter and Sharief that they were free to leave. The Commissioner told Hunter and Sharief to wait for him outside.

When everyone left, the Commissioner of Police spoke to Captain Rahman in a stern voice, "What were you doing aiding a Russian agent?"

Captain Rahman became very pale and replied, "I did not know she was a Russian agent. there"

"We will see," the Commissioner angrily said, "And one other thing, anytime someone is with me and you have an interrogation question, you ask the questions through me. Is that clear?"

"Yes sir," the captain replied.

The Commissioner went to the café door and spoke to Hunter and Sharief.

Hunter said to the Commissioner, "I've got to go back into the office to get the key."

"Let's go," the Commissioner replied, "I had a talk with the captain about his friendship with the Russian agent. By the way thanks for saving my life in there."

"You are very welcome Commissioner." Hunter replied

Hunter and Sharief followed the Commissioner toward the office. On the way they saw the captain, who was very apologetic and said, "Mr. Hunter and Mr. Sharief, if I have caused you any inconvenience I apology for that. I hope that you will forgive me."

"No problem." Hunter assured him.

They went into the office. The bodies were still there. The lab technicians and homicide detectives had not yet arrived. Hunter quickly removed the loose brick from behind the cabinet, but the key was not there. Hunter assumed that Nitasha had taken the key.

"Why didn't you give me the key?" the Commissioner questioned.

"If you check your pockets," Hunter noted, "You would find out that someone has already gone through your pockets."

Sharief and the Commissioner checked their pockets. To their surprise they noticed a few things rearranged. They realized that it could have been the Russian agent, Nitasha, who had gone through their pockets while they were hiding in the office.

❈   ❈   ❈

Hunter and Sharief decided to go to the Central Train Station where the locker was because they knew that Nitasha's next move was to take out the contents from the locker that matched the key number as soon as possible. The Commissioner dropped them off at the station and told them to call him if they needed his help. Hunter and Sharief got out of the car and walked quickly toward the locker area.

It was getting light, the sun was coming out. Hunter spotted Nitasha. She had a straw hat and was carrying a big handbag. She looked like a tourist coming back from a shopping spree. She walked nonchalantly toward the lockers, opened a locker and pulled out a brown leather briefcase. She walked quickly toward the stairs that went toward the exit platform.

Hunter saw Bernard DeLoatch, and two of his gang members, moving toward Nitasha Brincheska. A train was leaving the platform. Nitasha climbed onto the train instead of exiting the station. Bernard DeLoatch and his gang members caught the train as did Hunter and Sharief.

DeLoatch, and his cohorts, pushed passengers out of their way to follow Nitasha Brincheska, who had disappeared in the morning rush crowd. Hunter realized that Nitasha must have had a change of clothes in her handbag and changed into something new. Hunter noticed a slight built, fair young man, with a thin mustache, wearing army fatigues and an army hat. He moved pass them, going the opposite way. He had a big backpack on his back. Hunter noticed the young man's striking, hazel eyes when he passed; Hunter recognized those eyes anywhere. Hunter stopped Sharief, who had also recognized Nitasha in the army fatigues. She passed Bernard DeLoatch and his gang members, who did not recognized her and still headed in the wrong direction. Hunter knew that it was just matter of time before they would realize that they have lost track of Nitasha and double back, searching carefully, and maybe recognizing her disguise. Hunter would have loved to just let Nitasha slip through and see Bernard DeLoatch defeated but the information was just too important to let go.

Nitasha sat down about four rows ahead of Hunter and Sharief, near the exit. She leaned against a window seat in such a way that enabled her to observe train traffic from both directions. She was patiently waiting for the train to reach a station, any station—to get off.

DeLoatch and his henchmen returned. This time they looked at each and every passenger carefully. When Nitasha noticed them coming back she quickly got up and started moving toward the rear section of the train.

Sharief started to follow her but Hunter stopped him and said, "We don't want to be caught in the middle when bullets start flying." Sharief nodded and stayed where he was.

DeLoatch recognized Nitasha about ten rows away from him. He pointed toward Nitasha to show his companions where she was. They were now in hot pursuit of Nitasha Brincheska. Hunter and Sharief followed at a distance.

Nitasha reached the cargo cars where there weren't any passengers. Nitasha was one car ahead of DeLoatch and his henchmen. She jumped to the next open cargo car in front of her that had big pipes and heavy machinery parts covered with a thick canvas. There was a lot of room to hide. Hunter thought to himself that he would have made the same selection if he were in her shoes.

Nitasha did not look nervous or confused. She took every step with a calculated precision. This is why she was considered one of the best in the business of espionage; always in control to make the best possible choice against all odds. That is what separated her from the rest.

DeLoatch directed his men to go around the big pipes to trap her from both sides. One of DeLoatch's men started to climb over the big pieces of machinery parts to catch Nitasha unguarded. The other man went around with his gun drawn. DeLoatch stayed where he was, observing her from far away. He knew how dangerous his opponent was. He had told his men not to move in too fast, but he could see that they ignored his advice. They were careless and acted "macho." Hunter knew that the man who was climbing on the big pieces of machinery was headed for his doom. Being more in numbers does not mean that one should be careless when going against the best agent, like Nitasha Brincheska.

The man had barely reached the top when a shot rang out. The man's head jerked back as a bullet hit him in the forehead. He fell with a scream as his body rolled down the thick canvas and off of the train.

The other gangster started shooting repeatedly. DeLoatch was now right behind his man shooting at her. Nitasha was shooting back. Nitasha turned around and moved back toward the passenger cars with an amazing agility. Hunter and Sharief observed all this from the last passenger car before the cargo cars. The second henchman got over-zealous and careless in trying to overtake Nitasha as she carefully moved to cross the attachment between the cars.

She leaped over the attachment and grabbed the support handlebars of the last passenger car, which was empty, except for Hunter and Sharief. Nitasha, while dangling and holding onto the handlebars with one hand, shot the second henchman as he tried to follow Nitasha, falling off of the train. Nitasha, still dangling on the handlebars, tried to get a better grip when her gun fell out of her hand and fell under the train.

She tried to lift her body up to put her feet on the foothold of the passenger train, but the sweat on her palms and the rocky movements of the train made it difficult for her to lift her body and get in the passenger car. DeLoatch realizing her situation came out of hiding and started shooting at Nitasha. At this point, Hunter told Sharief to cover him. While Hunter helped pull Nitasha up, Sharief shot at DeLoatch, who cursed and ran back to take cover. Hunter pulled Nitasha in, grinned and said, "We better stop meeting like this."

Nitasha smiled and said, "Thank you."

"Let me lighten your burden," Hunter said, as he took the backpack off of her shoulders feeling a briefcase in her backpack that she had probably taken from the train station locker. Hunter moved the backpack safely closer to himself and away from Nitasha's reach.

"How generous of you to take the weight off my shoulders," she purred.

Hunter bowed and grinned. She did not seem bitter or upset as she sat down, leaned back, took a deep breath and closed her eyes.

Sharief and DeLoatch had stopped shooting at each other, but Sharief was keeping an eye on the open cargo car where DeLoatch hid behind heavy machinery.

Nitasha opened her eyes and Hunter said, "Are you tired?"

"Tired is not the word for it. I am fatigued."

"Then you are dressed appropriately," Hunter said looking at her army fatigues. She wore a navy blue suit under her army fatigue outfit. Nitasha reached into her little side kit. Hunter and Sharief stayed alert in case she pulled out a weapon, but when she pulled out a comb, a little mirror and a bottle of spray perfume and started combing her hair, Hunter and Sharief relaxed.

Nitasha smiled and said, "I hope you don't mind me fixing my hair. We girls have to look pretty."

"Not at all," Hunter replied.

Sharief whispered under his breath, "Women!"

Nitasha spoke again, "Mr. Hunter, I am grateful for your help. I don't know how to thank you."

Hunter grinned and smiled, "Let me spell out the ways you can thank me."

Nitasha smiled again as she picked up her perfume and sprayed it on her neck. Then quickly she sprayed it in Hunter's face. He caught the full spray in his face, and was blinded and dizzy. He yelled and sagged back in his seat.

Sharief was busy watching DeLoatch when he heard Hunter yell. By the time Sharief turned around to see what was going on, Nitasha grabbed Sharief's hand and with one karate chop near the shoulder broke his grip on his gun. She sprayed the same perfume in Sharief's face, and he sagged to the floor. She picked up Sharief's gun, took off the army fatigues, took the brief case out of the backpack and kicked the backpack and uniform under the seats. In her navy blue suit, she looked like a businesswoman. It all happened very fast.

DeLoatch watched what was going on from where he was hiding. He saw Nitasha with a briefcase that maybe contained the map. The train stopped on a busy station. DeLoatch took a few shots at Nitasha, who fired back. She quickly got off the train.

The train station was crawling with policemen on the platform. The train crew must have alerted the police. DeLoatch jumped off of the cargo car and followed Nitasha. She moved quickly through the station crowded with passengers and business people. DeLoatch did not notice Nitasha take off her blue suit jacket and throw it in a wastebasket. By the time DeLoatch reached the wastebasket where she had left her jacket, Nitasha had already double backed and passed him, and left the train station. When DeLoatch looked around he could find no sign of Nitasha Brincheska.

As the train stopped Hunter and Sharief regained their senses. Hunter checked Sharief's arm. It was badly broken. Hunter helped Sharief and they got off of the train. They called a cab and went to the embassy where a medic was waiting for Sharief.

*   *   *

Hunter went to his room, took a long bath and went to bed. It was late afternoon, when Hunter woke up with a telephone call. Ms Jennie Bain was on the line, "Hunter, are you still in bed?"

"Are you checking up on me, Mon Cherie?"

"That's my job," Ms. Jennie Bain replied, "Hunter, Mr. G. wants you to come here to the Cairo branch office in one hour. There are some strange things going on over here, so you better get here fast."

"Well then, I shall see you soon, Mon Cherie." Hunter quickly got ready and reported to Mr. Grace's office. It was not far away; Mr. Grace used it when he was in the Middle East.

Ms. Jennie Bain was at her desk looking at the computer screen. Hunter walked in and like a rogue chimed, "So you finally decided to chase me across the sea, halfway around the world." He placed a box of chocolates on her desk as he had often done.

Ms. Bain looked up. She was happy to see him and said mockingly, "Thank you for the chocolates. You know I will follow you, any time, any day, but right now you better hurry in. They are waiting for you."

As Hunter entered the office, for a moment he was surprised, then he quickly regained his composer. Inside the office, Mr. Grace, Dr. Fraction, the KGB Chief, Nitasha Brincheska, and a man he did not know were busy in discussion. The briefcase Nitasha has taken from the train station was lying on the table and Dr. Fraction was using a miniature x-ray analyzer to examine it.

Mr. Grace saw Hunter and said, "Hunter I want you to meet KGB Chief Salisnakoff, Agent Brincheska and Professor Yori, and of course you know Dr. Fraction." Everyone smiled and nodded hello. Mr. Grace added, "Due to the seriousness of the matter at hand, our governments have decided to work together on this project. Chief Salisnakoff and Agent Brincheska have provided us with the briefcase that contains the map of the whereabouts of the alien technology."

Hunter asked, "Why isn't the Russian government going to use the information on their own? They have the map."

The KGB Chief interjected, "Let me answer that."

Mr. Grace said, "Go ahead."

The KGB Chief continued, "There are many reasons. The first reason—with the recent breakup of our republic our resources are limited and we could not complete this operation in a proper manner. My superiors and I believe that there are many powerful adversaries still out there who will continue to pursue their quest to retrieve the alien technology at any cost. They would not stop just because we have the map. But if we work together we have a better chance of finding the artifacts, and most importantly, safely bringing it back. Second reason—We do not have the right combination to open this briefcase in order to get to the map."

He pointed to Dr. Fraction and continued, "Dr. Fraction can explain that to you better than I can."

Dr. Fraction said, "Observe." He turned on a scanning device, which had a screen. It showed a three-dimensional image of the contents of the brief case. They could see the parchment that was rolled up. Alongside of it there seemed to be a crude bomb that occupied the rest of the briefcase. We need the correct combination to open the briefcase. If we use a wrong combination or any electronic device to find the correct combination it could trigger the bomb and destroy the map, not to mention injure others close by."

Mr. Grace said, "Colonel Brincheska has reason to believe that you have the correct combination."

"What makes her so certain that I have the combination?" questioned Hunter.

The KGB Chief said, "Agent Nitasha can explain."

"Certainly," Nitasha said, "The day the owner of the Sand Rock Café was killed, Mr. Hunter was one of the people who first entered the office after the commotion. One of our agents saw him take something off of the owner's upper arm. The coroners noticed a very distinct indentation mark around the dead man's upper arm, made by a string and a small square object about the size of a locket. Many people in this part of the world wear such lockets called 'tavecz,' which they believe bring blessings and good fortune. The locket was never found. We checked with some of the employees, who mentioned that they had heard the owner say that there were good luck numbers in that locket that were going to bring him good fortune. I believe that he was talking about those combination numbers and, I believe, Mr. Hunter has them."

The KGB chief smiled admiringly at Nitasha and said, "With our joint efforts, I am certain that we will succeed."

Hunter took out a small folded paper from his pocket; "This is the paper, which I removed from the locket. It does have numbers on it. Would you like me to try them out on the briefcase?"

Mr. Grace said, "Go ahead, Hunter"

Hunter entered the combination numbers and after a few tries the briefcase clicked open. Mr. Grace gently picked up the parchment from the briefcase. Dr. Fraction gave the briefcase to one of his assistants to disconnect the wires from the bomb and destroy the bomb. Among the parchments was a map, which Dr. Fraction and Professor Yori carefully spread on a large table. The papyrus parchment was still in fairly good shape. It was a crude handmade map with notations and some writings on the bottom. Dr. Fraction magnified the map. Professor Yori studied the writings and various locations on the map. Dr. Fraction helped Professor Yori write down the translation of the writings on the map. With the passing of thousands of years the names and the geographical shapes of many places on the map had changed. Professor Yori and Dr. Fraction converted the translations to present day locations.

Professor Yori said, "According to the map, the artifacts along with the treasures are buried in the desert in a mountainous area. The main starting point is the sphinx. The writings say that a four-man party was given responsibility to hide and bury the treasure. They got up at sunrise and started their journey moving along with the rise of the sun, moving in a straight line in the direction away from the sphinx. As they were directed, according to these writings, they traveled forty miles until they reached a hill. At the foot step of the hill there was a water well and a small oasis. If you stand on that hill, about a mile away they saw three small hills. The hill on your far right had a cavern. That is the cavern where the box of knowledge is hidden.

"The entrance of the cavern was blocked off with big rocks and sticker bushes. Unless you are specifically looking for the cavern the area looks like a part of solid rock. You can not find the hidden cavern easily because the foothills are miles and miles long. According to the map you look for a monadnock, which is simply the hardest core of a hill or a mountain or a hill left behind after it disintegrated because of erosion. You will stand on the monadnock facing the foot of the hill. The cavern is twenty-five yards away from there."

"Extraordinary work, Professor Yori," an impressed Dr. Fraction said, "Of course it has been thousands of years. It could be a very difficult task to find the entrance to the cavern because we don't know how much sand and other materials have been deposited there. Archaeologists will have to be called in to carefully excavate the area."

Mr. Grace and the KGB Chief did not seem to like the idea of bringing in archaeologists. Mr. Grace spoke, "We can not bring in archaeologists for a full excavation, because it would require permission from the sovereign government letting them know what and why we are excavating the area. At the end they will be in there right to keep the finding in their country. That is why we are sending Hunter and Nitasha as a team of two to independently find the exact location and then if need be to send in a small force, get the artifacts and get out of there."

The KGB Chief added, "I fully agree with Mr. Grace." He then asked Professor Yori, "You are a world re-known archaeologist, how deep do you think the treasure would be buried?"

Professor Yori replied, "Well, by studying the location of the hill that has the artifact, and the two other surrounding hills and a fourth hill in front of these hills—this will considerably block and minimize the sand and other materials being deposited in front of the entrance because the hills would block the wind storms, in my opinion."

Mr. Grace said, "If need be we will have a team of army archaeologists excavators at the ready when the location of the cavern has been determined."

Professor Yori continued, "These writings are extraordinary in their detail. You enter the cavern, which is about two miles long. There are cliffs and stalagmites in the cavern. There are deep, bottomless cracks in the rocks. It will probably be slippery in there, so walk very carefully. The writings say that at the end of the cavern will be a triangle carved in the rock pointing down. Below is an opening in the rock where the treasure can be found. It is blocked by other rocks, which will have to be removed.

"The map was drawn after the cavern was chosen and inspected by a handful of leaders. They determined where to safely bury the treasure before sending the four well respected and trustworthy young men. Once they came with the news that the treasures were successfully hidden, minor adjustments were made on the map and the only copy was kept in a safe place with the parchments."

"Thank you, again Professor Yori," Dr. Fraction said, "I would like to add that there is a comment on the bottom of the map. It reads 'A word to the wise. The terrain in the cavern is treacherous. Watch your step and control your greed.' Now remember in those days when the treasures or valuables were buried they were buried in an area which was difficult and naturally dangerous to reach, so be very careful."

"Thank you Professor Yori and Dr. Fraction," Roger Grace said, "I am so glad that our governments have realized that the world would be a better place if we collaborate on these important missions rather that compete.

"I agree," The KGB Chief said, "We can accomplish so much more working together. Now, let me tell you of an important device we have developed. It is a miniature precious metal detecting device. It will be placed in Agent Nitasha's bracelet. This device could home in on the location of gold and silver treasures, which had been buried with the artifacts."

"That will be very useful," Mr. Grace said, "I would like Hunter and Nitasha to know that we will be in constant touch. Any signs of trouble, I will have the air sport immediately dispatched. Dr. Fraction has made some adjustments to the All Terrain Transport that you will be using. He will go over that with you."

✤   ✤   ✤

After the meeting Nitasha asked the KGB Chief about André, her assistant who was keeping surveillance on the Sand Rock Café with her. The KGB Chief made a few calls and said to Nitasha:

"The young man left a message that he was going to the apartment to dismantle the surveillance equipment. It was about an hour ago." Nitasha looked worried, got up and said,

"He should not go there. His life is in danger because DeLoatch and his henchmen will be looking for me, and the apartment is the first place they will start." She called the apartment but there was no answer. She got up and said, "I've got to go to the apartment. There is not a moment to lose."

Hunter got up with Nitasha and said, "I will go with you."

"O.K. Let's go."

Hunter and Nitasha left the office and met Ms. Jenni Bain in the hallway. She said to Nitasha, "Oh, there you are. Hello, Ms. Brincheska."

Nitasha quickly said hello and passed by, while Ms. Jenni Bain whispered to Hunter, "Does she ever smile?"

"She is in a hurry," Hunter said, "I will explain it to you later. Please call the Commissioner of Police and tell him that I would like him to meet me at Nitasha's apartment immediately."

Hunter caught up with Nitasha and got into Nitasha's car. When they arrived at the apartment Nitasha got out of the car and was at the apartment door before Hunter could get out of the car. The apartment door was unlocked. Nitasha ran up the stairs without making a noise.

Two big hooded men had tied André to a chair and were interrogating him about Nitasha. Their backs were toward the door. André was badly beaten. He seemed unconscious. One man said to the other man, "He does not know anything. Just waste him and let's get out of here." The other big man lifted his hand with a metal object and was ready to strike André when Nitasha moved and grabbed his raised hand, twisted it backward and broke his arm. The man fell backward in pain. The second man threw a punch at Nitasha, which she blocked with her hand, but which knocked the gun out of her hand. With a knife drawn the man lunged at Nitasha. She sprang to one side and kicked the knife out of his hand. The man with the broken arm had taken a gun out when Hunter entered the room. Hunter kicked the gun out of his hand. The uninjured man fled the room, leaving the man with the broken arm alone.

Nitasha called the ambulance, untied André and made him sit comfortably in the chair while she gently wiped the blood from his face and forehead. He regained consciousness and was pleased to see Nitasha, and surprised to see Hunter. Nitasha read his expression and told him that Hunter was there to help, which put Andre's mind at ease. André wanted to get up but Nitasha told him to rest until the ambulance came.

The Commissioner of Police arrived when the ambulance did. Hunter relayed what happened. One of the police officers took off the mask of the gangster and the Commissioner of Police said that the man was one of a local small time hoodlum gang. "He reached the end of his rope," the Commissioner said, "He's going to be locked up for a long time."

The attacker cursed his friend who got him involved and left him while he was injured.

Hunter and Nitasha returned to Mr. Grace's Middle Eastern branch office. Ms. Jenni Bain told them that Mr. Grace and Dr. Fraction were waiting for them.

Mr. Grace said, "Hunter, Brincheska, Dr. Fraction will go over some instruction and adjustments he made to the all terrain transport that you will be using for the mission. Good luck."

"Follow me, please," Dr. Fraction said.

Nitasha asked, "Do you want me wait while you speak to Hunter?"

"No. My instructions are to provide all information and details to both of you."

They followed Dr. Fraction to the vehicle. Dr. Fraction pointed to the vehicle and said, "This vehicle is bulletproof. It can move in the desert and mountainous terrain as well as it does on the road."

Hunter queried, "You mean to say that I can run this car 100 mile per hour on the road and I can run it with the same speed and with the same ease in the desert and the mountainous terrain?"

Dr. Fraction hesitated and said, "Well, of course it will run differently on different terrain. What I am trying to say is that it will also ride comfortably in the desert and mountainous terrain."

Hunter smiled and replied, "Why did you not say so in the first place?"

Dr. Fraction ignored Hunter's interruption and continued, "The car's camouflage paint allows it to easily blend in with the desert sand."

He pointed toward a red button on the control panel and said, "Once this red button is pressed, it will release a covering that will cover the car and make it look like a small sand dune. Once covered you will still be able to see out because the material is translucent. Press the red button three times and the covering will be retracted.

"The vehicle is air-conditioned even when it is not running. You can run this vehicle indefinitely. It runs on solar power and a miniature plutonium chip."

Hunter pointed to four buttons on the panel and asked, "What is the function of these buttons?"

"The white button allows the radio to change into a two-way radio transmitter. To change it back to a radio, press the white button three times. The blue button is use to operate two high-powered machine guns in the back of the car. The barrels are located behind your license plate numbers 0-1-0. If you look closely at those zeros, these are the barrels of your machine guns. The orange button is to operate two machine guns in front. The green button is to send an S-O-S signal in case your radio frequency is jammed. These S-O-S signals can be picked up by any navy vessel or land base and carry an immediate and urgent response code."

Hunter asked, "Suppose I lose the keys? What do I do?"

"In case you lose your keys, put you right thumb on the door lock on the driver side and do the same for the ignition to turn the car on and drive.

"Now if I may continue. If you press the purple button on the joystick on the panel it will lock onto a target and fire a missile. You have six missiles mounted on the rooftop of your vehicle.

"There is a refrigerator filled with nutritious food, enough to last for four weeks. The water supply is plenty, but use it carefully."

Hunter asked, "How long will the water last?"

"The water supply lines are connected to condensers that extract water from the nighttime air. Nighttime air in the desert is cold and moist.

"I have placed an instruction manual, along with all the pertinent information, in the glove compartment. If you still have a question, use the transmitter and I will assist you. Take good care of this vehicle."

Hunter tapped the car and as Dr. Fraction winced said, "We'll do."

Hunter and Nitasha wanted to inspect the vehicle so while Dr. Fraction observed they got into the vehicle to check it out. They found it spacious and comfortable. When they got out Hunter slammed the door shut, which upset Dr. Fraction and he said, "Hunter, could you for once try to be a little careful?"

While they were inspecting the car Mr. Grace and Ms. Jenni Bain came to the garage with two big suitcases in back of a golf cart that they were driving. The suitcases contained special clothing for desert travel and all the necessary items for daily use.

That night Hunter and Nitasha were to stay in the guest rooms at Mr. Grace's Middle Eastern branch office, and the plan was that the next day in the morning they would slip in with the other traffic and start their journey.

❧   ❧   ❧

The next day everyone was up before dawn. Hunter and Nitasha were dressed in desert robes and had headpieces on to cover their hair, protecting them from the desert heat and also disguising their European looks. It was hard to determine by their dress that Nitasha was a female.

The air was cool, early in the morning when Hunter and Nitasha said their good-byes and got into the all terrain transport vehicle. The hot sun had not yet graced the skies. All their necessary supplies had been packed. As they started to drive the vehicle, many locals were also starting their cars to begin their work commutes. The traffic was still light on the roads which helped them to move fast.

Their departure did not go unnoticed. A short, stocky man, who was one of Kavanaugh's hoodlums, observed them across the highway. He had been watching their every move with a high-powered telescope from the window of a store across from Mr. Grace's Middle-Eastern branch office compound. The short, stocky man picked up the phone and dialed a number and said, "This is Kraven, give me Mr. Kavanaugh."

Usually it was difficult to reach Kavanaugh on the phone, but the call went through quickly. Kavanaugh was on the line, "Yes Kraven, do you have something for me?"

"The American agent and the Russian agent had just left their office compound and the way they were dressed and packed and the direction they were headed, it looks like they are prepared for a long journey, traveling through the deep desert."

Mr. Kavanaugh replied, "Good job, now clear out of the building. Make sure that there is no trace of any evidence that you were ever there."

It was still early in the morning when Hunter and Nitasha reached the Sphinx. There were tourist groups who were also starting desert trips. Hunter and Nitasha blended in with the tourists, and started their quest.

❦   ❦   ❦

Early in the morning Bernard DeLoatch walked into Cavanaugh's office; Cavanaugh did not look very happy. Cavanaugh spoke in admonishing, but civil manner; he did not want to anger the notorious smuggler, Bernard DeLoatch. "Well Bernard, so far you have been reckless and been outsmarted by the American agents. As of now I want you to follow my plan. I have been keeping an eye on the activities of the American and Russian agents. My sources have informed me that the Americans and Russians have joined forces and are working together. I do not like this development. I am also informed that the American agent and the Russian agent are headed into the deep desert in an 'all-terrain vehicle,' as they call it."

"I'll take care of it," DeLoatch interjected, "My associates are also watching the American and Russian agents."

Curtly, Cavanaugh said, "Listen, I want you to personally take charge of this mission from now on. I do not want it be handled by second string operatives." More calmly, Cavanaugh continued, "Now remember we have missed our advantage of getting our hands on the map and getting to the artifact first. Now we have no choice but to mingle with the other tourist groups and follow the American and Russian agents. They will lead us to the artifacts. Once they have retrieved the artifact and it is in their possession, only then do you take the agents, and get rid of them. Make sure that your men don't jump the gun and jeopardize the outcome of the mission."

"I'll get on it right away," DeLoatch said, "But you do realize that the American and Russian agents will know that they are being tracked. In the open desert you can not hide."

"Of course they will know that they are being watched," Cavanaugh snapped, "But they also want to work secretively to retrieve the artifacts. If the ruling government of the land finds out what is going on they can easily claim the artifact as their national property and take ownership of the artifact. The American and Russian agents want to keep it quiet. They don't want to create an incident. All parties will work secretively. Do you understand …? Now, I want you to prepare for a deep desert expedition, use your resources to the maximum, expense is no problem, but get me the artifacts; do not disappoint me."

Hunter and Nitasha had been traveling for a few hours. Many groups that started out with them had left and gone to there planned exploration routes. The desert and sand dunes were all around them. They saw an endless sea of sand as far as there sight could reach. It was beautiful and serene. Occasionally a rocky hill, desert plants or shrubbery appeared, defying the scorching desert. Three more hours passed by and now they were the only travelers as far as they could see.

They both knew that it was just a matter of time before Cavanaugh, and DeLoatch's gangsters came into the picture. Cavanaugh, with all his means, would not give up easily. Cavanaugh and DeLoatch were smart thugs. They had been burnt once by losing the map, but they wouldn't make that mistake again. Hunter and Nitasha had a hunch that they would not be confronted with Cavanaugh and DeLoatch until they retrieved the artifact.

They did not come across any caravans or traveling nomads, which was expected as the path that Hunter and Nitasha were traveling was not a common route. Perhaps the people who chose the hiding place for the artifacts and treasures thousands of years ago knew that this area was going to be avoided by generations to come. They went deeper into the desert. The area was known to have an abundance of deadly scorpions and side winders.

The all-terrain vehicle was equipped with adjustable inner binoculars, high powered scopes to view the front, rear, above and side of the vehicle for observation and surveillance. Hunter was driving, and Nitasha was using the equipment to observe the surroundings. It was comfortable, as the sun had gone down. The vehicle was also equipped with the GPS tracking system.

"Do you see anything?" Hunter asked Nitasha.

"Nothing yet. I don't see anyone following us, but it is too soon to tell."

Adjusting the radar screen Hunter said, "Looks like it is going to be a long stretch."

Carefully, Nitasha said, "Well, according to the map it is going to take two days' journey to reach the target area where the artifacts are buried, I don't foresee any action until these two days have passed." Contradicting her prediction, the all-terrain vehicle came to an abrupt stop, and the wheels spun in place as the vehicle started to sink. "We drove into quicksand," Nitasha calmly stated, "I hope Dr. Fraction's equipment works."

"It will work," Hunter replied as he quickly turned a dial and pressed a button. With a quiet humming, a cushiony air-filled panel stretched underneath and on the sides of the vehicle. Hunter turned a throttle located near the gear shift handle. The vehicle lifted above the ground and started gliding forward on a cushion of air; flew over the quicksand. He landed the vehicle, pressed a switch, and the all-terrain vehicle made a low humming sound as the cushiony panel deflated and folded back underneath the vehicle. The vehicle was now back on wheels.

They got out and checked the vehicle. There was no damage; everything was in perfect condition. So far, all the equipment in the vehicle had worked perfectly. Although Hunter made light humor of Dr. Fraction's scientific equipment—deep—down he trusted what Dr. Fraction issued. Many times his life depended on Dr. Fraction's equipment and it always came through. It was Hunter who had started calling Dr. Fraction, Dr. Fraction, and the name stuck.

Nitasha and Hunter decided to stretch and walk around a little. Nitasha told Hunter that she studied plants, as she collected some deep desert plant and vegetation samples. They returned to the vehicle and this time Nitasha took the driver's seat, and as it was getting dark they decided to find a place to spend the night.

Nitasha saw a little hill a few hundred yards ahead and as she drove closer she said, "This hill looks like a good spot to spend night. It will provide protection from the sand blowing in the air and piling up on us and burying us under a sand dune." Hunter agreed, and they drove up the side of the hill. Nitasha found a clear spot and stopped. They surveyed their surroundings and not seeing anyone they pressed a camouflage buttons to make the vehicle look like a little sandy hill. Once the vehicle was camouflaged, inner lights came on. These lights could not be seen from the outside. The vehicle was sound proof, as well. Inside was very spacious for two people to board comfortably.

Once situated Hunter used a special transmitter in the vehicle that had a frequency that could only be received at the Global Intelligence Services Headquarters. A secretary received the transmissions, and immediately notified Mr. Grace, Chief of GIS. Mr. Grace and Dr. Fraction had been waiting for his call.

Mr. Grace asked, "How are things going?"

"Everything is proceeding smoothly," Hunter replied, "We should be at our target sight according to our plans."

Dr. Fraction asked, "I have monitored your progress in the all-terrain vehicle and was pleased to see that it got you out of the quicksand. The equipment in the vehicle was tested and double tested by me, so you and agent Nitasha, should not encounter any problems with it."

Before Hunter could reply, Mr. Grace interjected, "By the way, we have picked up two groups of travelers which are trailing about two miles behind you and they are about one mile apart from each other. We have picked up their transmissions. They are Bernard DeLoatch and his mercenaries working for Cavanaugh. Each group is made out of twenty people. So the minute you have the artifact in your possession let us know and our air force and paratroopers will get you out of there in a matter of minutes. I don't think Bernard DeLoutch and his hoodlums will make any move before that, but we are ready never-the-less, in case they decide to do something foolish and jump the gun."

Hunter noticed two dots on the tracking screen, which meant the two groups of travelers about two miles from them. Hunter replied, "We are observing them also on our tracking screen. They were not there a few hours ago. Someone must have air transported them when it got dark to not to raise any suspicion. We will keep you informed about any new developments."

Hunter and Nitasha observed the two groups quietly as Hunter zoomed in on one of the groups. The screen showed about twenty men, all dressed in budueen robes. But when they looked carefully they could see that under their common desert clothing they were dressed in fatigues and were armed with state-of-the-art weapons. They looked and moved like trained fighting men. Hunter Nitasha watched as the group set up camp. Their camp was neatly arranged with lines of rugged convoy vehicles with heavy duty mortar weapons. There were trailers loaded with grenade launchers and assault rifles. All the vehicles and weapons were care-fully camouflaged. They had enough fire power to fight an army. They also had camels that surrounded the camp. That was clever because to untrained eyes they looked like a cara-van of nomads.

Bernard DeLoatch called this group the "Ground Attack Unit". The leader of the ground attack was a big, rugged European man called "Big Tom". Big Tom, a mean and nasty fellow, was always proud of his long association with Ber-nard DeLoatch. Big Tom's men were intimidated by him. If Big Tom had to kill someone, he never gave it a second thought or showed remorse. Big Tom would kill anyone who got in his way, no matter how close he was to them.

The second group that Hunter and Nitasha observed was called the "Air Assault Unit". Bernard DeLoatch was person-ally in-charge of this group. This group, also armed with state of the art weapons, had helicopters and small fighter planes.

As aggressive as these two groups appeared, Hunter and Natasha were also aware that their vehicle was capable of fighting a small army. They would be able to hold off the attackers until help arrived.

Not worried about the two groups camping nearby Hunter and Nitasha ate there dinner in the rear part of the vehicle where there was a dinning area, and then got ready to sleep. Natasha turned on the surveillance and motion detec-tors to detect anything which came closer then twenty yard from the vehicle. Hunter asked Nitasha, if she would like to join him for a glass of wine but Nitasha said politely that the wine often made her sleepy and she wanted to be alert in case something comes up during the night.

Nitasha went to one of the big chairs right behind the driver seat and pressed some levers and it slid into a comfortable bed as a thick patrician curtain dropped from the roof of the vehicle giving Nitasha privacy as she changed to go to sleep. Hunter turned off the inner lights, except the night lights, pressed some levers on the second seat that changed into a bed and he lay down.

They had been sleeping for a few hours when a sharp ringing sound of the alarm woke them. Hunter got up and looked at the night vision screens; Nitasha right beside him. Hunter and Nitasha could see two figures crouching and moving toward the hill where the vehicle was camouflaged. One man was the Ground Attack Unit leader, Big Tom The two men were crouching and very carefully moving toward the vehicle.

The two men were so close to the vehicle that sensors picked up their voices. "Where could they have gone?" the big man said to a shorter guy, as he adjusted his night vision goggles, "We have been watching them constantly.... We saw them going behind that little hill. Then they just disappeared into thin air." They continued to search. "I am telling you, they are hiding somewhere very close."

The shorter man replied, "Let's get out of here. You told me that we were just going to poke around for a short while. DeLoatch is not going to like this a bit. His orders were very specific; no one was to go looking for those agents. We were to keep a two-mile distance from them, until DeLoatch gives the orders to move in."

Big Tom huffed, "Who is going to tell him?"

"No one has to tell him. DeLoatch has ways. He probably knows by now what we are doing," the smaller man replied, "He has his informers."

Ignoring this warning, Big Tom adjusted his night vision goggles hoping to spot the vehicle. He did not see anything, uttered some profanities and reluctantly agreed to turn back.

After listening to those intruders, Hunter said, "This reaffirms our theory that DeLoatch and his mercenaries will not attack until we have retrieved the artifacts."

Nitasha added, "We will have very little time, if any, to get away, once we find the artifacts, before DeLoatch and his men arrive."

The rest of the night passed without incident, and before dawn Hunter pressed a switch that retracted the desert camouflage from the all-terrain vehicle. When Hunter drove the vehicle down the hill they were back on the surveillance grids of their pursuers.

Hunter and Nitasha studied the built-in compass screen on their desert quadrant map grid that Professor Yori and Dr. Fraction made for them. The map was amazingly precise, making navigating the desert easy, however Nitasha kept a watch on the monitors surveying the surroundings for quicksand in their path. They did not pick up transmissions from DeLoatch and his men. Hunter and Nitasha knew that they were being followed because they monitored them on their monitoring grid. They could see Bernard DeLoatch on the monitors, in the lead helicopter, followed by two helicopters, leading his trained murderers.

The two groups of Bernard DeLoatch's mercenaries, (the Ground Attack Unit and the Air Assault Unit) continued to follow Nitasha and Hunter at a two-mile distance, as the desert sun steadily climbed in the desert skies. It was beginning to get uncomfortably hot so Hunter closed the windows and Nitasha turned the air conditioner on.

About two mile away, Bernard DeLoatch's helicopter landed near the Ground Attack Unit, while the other two helicopters stayed in the air flying low to avoid radar detection. The sun had now raised the desert temperatures beyond human comfort, and the mercury was still steadily climbing. The Ground Attack Unit came to a halt as Bernard DeLoatch's helicopter landed.

Bernard DeLoatch, and two Burly European confidants, stepped out of the helicopter. The Ground Attack Unit leader, Tom, who still looked a little tired from his excursion the previous night, stepped toward them, smiled sheepishly and said, "Mr. DeLoatch, it's a pleasure to see you."

DeLoatch grinned, showing his teeth through thin red lips, like a wolf looking at his prey before attacking, "I want to speak to you. Let us go near the helicopter." The rugged and tough Big Tom showed signs of fear as he walked toward two burly men standing near the helicopter.

DeLoatch turned toward the Ground Attack Unit and said, "Wait for my orders to pull out." He called the shorter man over who had left the unit with Big Tom the night before. DeLoatch looked at the group of men. They were standing quietly, in a relaxed position, waiting for his order to move out. They did not seem concerned about their leader Big Tom, who had disobeyed Bernard DeLoatch. This eased DeLoatche's mind. He was a careful thug who did not underestimate any of his underlings. That is why he kept two gun-mounted helicopters circling in the air, in case the men in the Ground Attack Unit joined with Big Tom and rebelled against him. It seemed the rest of the men in Ground Attack Unit either did not care about their leader or were glad to see Big Tom get into trouble because he was not a well-liked person. Whichever it was, Deloatch wanted it that way. Everyone in the Ground Attack Unit was afraid of Bernard DeLoatch. They did not want his wrath to fall upon them.

When Big Tom was separated from the other men, the two burly companions of Bernard DeLoatch, who have stayed near the helicopter, moved on either side of Big Tom. DeLoatch ordered one of the burly men to take away Big Tom's weapons. The man thoroughly frisked him, even took his desert boots, to check for hidden weapons. He took away Big Tom's two guns and a dagger that he had always carried.

Once Big Tom was unarmed, Bernard DeLoatch said in a monotone voice, "Why did you disobey my strict orders and went looking for the American and Russian agents? And when someone tried to remind you about my orders you chose to disregard and forced him to follow you?' He pointed toward his companion. "Do you know that because of your reckless action you might have put the whole mission in jeopardy?"

Big Tom licking his dry lips to moisten them said, "I was just trying to help. I am sorry."

Bernard DeLoatch did not reply to Big Tom, instead he told Big Tom to take off his fatigues. Big Tom obeyed, and now he was standing in his boxer shorts that had clowns printed on them, which made one of the DeLoatch's lieutenant's laugh. Bernard DeLoatch growled, "Don't ever laugh at someone who had worked for me. What I am doing, I have to do. That does not mean that you show disrespect to him. Give his desert boots back and go get a jeep."

The man, immediately silenced, gave Big Tom his desert boots, and ran to get the jeep. Big Tom quickly put his boots on, hoping his life had been spared. The man came back with a jeep in no time.

Bernard DeLoatch told the short man, and Big Tom to get in. Big Tom obeyed as his body motions showed a combination of trembling and shaking. Bernard DeLoatch and his second lieutenant also climbed into the jeep. Everyone rode silently. The two helicopters followed the jeep closely. They drove about five miles away from the Ground Attack Unit when Bernard DeLoatch told them to stop. Bernard DeLoatch told Big Tom, "You have worked for me for a long time. Because of that I am not going to shoot you. Instead I am going to let you out here. If you reach your unit I will let you live but you will not be the leader of your unit." Then he told the driver of the jeep to turn around and head back to camp.

On the way back Bernard DeLoatch said to the short man, "I am appointing you the leader of the Ground Attack

Unit. Always keep me informed about what is going on and never disobey me."

The short man replied, "I will do exactly what you tell me. Thank you for giving me the command of Ground Attack Unit."

It was high noon, and the desert sun was now turning the desert into a crucible of fire. The newly appointed leader of the Ground Attack Unit could feel the particles of hot sand hitting like miniature brimstones on part of his face, which was not protected by goggles. He thought of the ex-leader, who did not have any protective goggles or clothing. He never liked him; he never liked Big Tom; he was always brash, unreasonable and uncooperative; he got what he deserved.

The jeep approached the Ground Attack Unit camp. Bernard DeLoatch, his two burly lieutenants and the short man stepped out of the jeep. All the men in the Ground Attack Unit stood up straight and attentive as Bernard DeLoatch spoke to them, "I am appointing Nicholas (he pointed toward the short man) your new leader. I want every one of you to listen to him. I want all of you to remember that any disobedience will not be tolerated. Once this mission is accomplished, you will be awarded generously in addition to your pay. Your new leader will give you directions."

Bernard DeLoatch, and his lieutenants, got into the helicopter and left along with the other two helicopters. The new leader, Nicholas, told the Ground Attack Unit members, "Follow me and keep the present distance from the American and Russian agents. Do not close in until I tell

you. Let us pull out." The men congratulated Nicholas; he
was a well-liked person. The Ground Attack Unit men got
into there jeeps and followed Nicholas.

It's been only one hour since the ex-leader, Big Tom, was
left in the burning desert to find his way back to camp. The
particles of hot burning sand hit his naked body—like hot,
little daggers from hell causing painful burns and blisters.
His eyes could hardly see. In order to save his eyes being hit
by sand particle he walked in the direction the wind was
blowing, which was the opposite direction of the camp. He
tried to wet his lips with his tongue but his tongue felt like a
hot dried piece of flesh, which made his already cracked,
blistering lips feel pangs of sharp pain. He tried to scream,
but only hoarse, gurgling noises came out of his throat. He
wanted to cry, but no tears could come out. As he looked
ahead he saw a shining pool of water far ahead of him. He
used his last ounce of strength and determination to stagger
toward that body of water. He did not pay attention to a
group of circling vultures, who had started to move closer
and closer to him. When Big Tom finally reached spot where
he saw the pool of water, he was surprised when the pool of
water moved further away. That made him lose all hope. He
screamed, but his screams only echoed in his head without
sounds, because his dried-up throat and mouth could not
form a sound. He cried, but no tears could form in his eyes.

The unfortunate, delirious man tripped on a little rock
and fell, which disturbed a nest of scorpions, hidden under
the rock for shelter from the burning sun. Big Tom did not
have the strength to stand up and walk, so he started to

crawl. The angry scorpions came out from underneath the rock and attacked the half-dead crawling man with a vengeance, as they stung him again and again. Big Tom's brain registered sharp pain on all over his body. He released a last quiet sigh in the scorching desert as his mind went blank and his all bodily functions ceased.

One of the vultures saw the man's body become still, and carefully came closer. It dug its beak into his neck, and when the man did not move it let out a loud squeal to alert the other vultures that it was safe to feast upon their prey. Within a matter of minutes, the whole group of hungry vultures bit away his flesh from Big Tom's bones. This was the end of a cruel gangster's life.

COMING SOON

MARAUDERS OF THE

ROSWELL LINKS
Episode II

Code name: Q F T A M C

Hunter and Nitasha had a good start. The new alliance between American agent, Hunter and Russian agent, Nitasha Brincheska meant that they would be working side-by-side. They must stay in close company throughout their mission. Hunter and Nitasha must race against time to find the alien technology before anyone else could get their hands on it. They have the map, now they must find the alien computer pieces, along with the extraterrestrial micro-chip made of a diamond-like substance. Hunter and Nitasha must find these artifacts and secure them before they fall into the wrong hands, which could spell destruction for the civilized world.

Printed in the United States
202983BV00001B/160-261/P